THE NUDE YARDMAN

The Nude Yardman

Stanford O'Neil

Christmas, Ranger & Light

Published by Christmas, Ranger and Light Media
476 Hopkins Crandall Road
Smyrna NY 13464

Copyright 2024 by
Phillip Ozdemir

ISBN: 979-8-9900470-0-6

LCCN: 2024902745

Published by arrangement with
Christmas, Ranger & Light Media
For information contact:
Christmas Ranger & Light
at the address above

First Printing, 2024

Life is either a daring adventure or nothing at all.
-Helen Keller

And the man and his wife were both naked and they
were not ashamed.
-Genesis 12:25

1

The Early Years

When the nude yardman was a little boy, he had the curious habit of going over to his grandmother's house and taking off all his clothes and helping her with the yard work. 'That boy is going to grow up to be a nude yardman', his grandmother used to say, watching him do this, and wondering about it, as people will wonder about the curious habits of others, especially those in their own families, even though, truth be known, the fact that she and others used to say it probably didn't have much to do with his choice of avocation, first of all because he was too young to understand what a 'yardman' was (when he first started this curious habit of his, he was only barely able to cut his own meat, for heaven's sake), and secondly, because nobody ever dared to say it in front of him. They always whispered it among themselves out of earshot, as people will do whenever they gossip about someone else. Of course, when they were saying this many, many years ago, it was a novel thing for them to say for no one had ever seen a yardman working in the nude before. All the yardmen that they knew, in that era, were always fully clothed. Well, maybe not always *fully* clothed, for there were always the yardmen who took their shirts off in the summer, and just wore shorts on hot days. But the time when nude yard workers had an absolute legal right to work in the buff, a right guaranteed by an Amendment to the Constitution, was still far in the future.

The nude yardman! Perhaps not since Jesus, or Mohammed or Philo Farnsworth has a single individual played such an important role in the affairs of men. Where does one begin to chronicle the life of such an extraordinary person? The normal course of a serious, comprehensive biography which would attempt to accurately and vividly trace the life of such an individual - who had such a far-reaching effect on the world, and on humanity in general - would be for the biographer to first off dutifully include details about the events and influences in his early life that contributed to his character. There would be the obligatory references to both his paternal and maternal grandparents, where they were born, and how they made their living, how that influenced the lives and upbringing of his parents, a detailed look at both of his parents, how they met, what they did, and how they influenced his ideas, personality and character. Then, of course, there would be a step-by-step, year-by-year history of his juvenile, and early adult years, culminating in a blow-by-blow account of the discontents, love-affairs, struggles and accomplishments of his adulthood. But we will not try to hew to this model too closely, alerting the reader that this is not a professionally authored biography as such, but merely an attempt to set down what facts about the nude yardman that the author can remember from his own contemporaneous knowledge of him, without the benefit of the extensive historical research facilities that might be available with a large staff and/or limitless financial resources of a major academic or philanthropic institution. And oh heck, biographies like that aren't much fun to read anyway, so we'll just tell the story as best as we can and hope you like it. So come along for the ride, gentle reader. We shall drift in and out of point of view and chronological sequence in the manner of Conrad, and hope that by doing so we shall give the reader a fair and more balanced sense of this extraordinary life.

To start off we would like to observe that while other individuals have attempted to make much of the fact that the nude yardman's paternal grandfather had been committed to a mental institution for a nervous breakdown in an attempt to lay the foundation for a plausible explanation of the nude yardman's peculiar behavior in a particular strain of mental illness which ran through his family, we feel such pundits miss the point in attempting to explain the nude yard worker movement from the point of view of an anomaly or aberration. Although such a point of view might have had some legitimacy in the early days of the movement, and perhaps in the early diagnosis of its progenitor's then curious acts - since, from the point of view of the norms of the day, such behavior as preparing the soil in the flower beds for a new flat of petunias, pushing the lawnmower around, or raking leaves entirely in the nude was, it must be admitted, somewhat exceptional - we now know, with the benefit of hindsight, and with the wholesome, heartwarming, absolutely overwhelming evidence of the popularity of the movement, first in our nation and then in others, that the desire to do yard work in the nude is most unexceptional. In fact we must admit, as have all other serious scholars who have studied this question, that it is a perfectly normal trait for human beings to want to do yard work in the nude, and those who do so live longer, better, more fulfilling lives. Their rates of cancer and heart disease are lower, their muscle tone is better, and their lifespan markedly improved. This has been established beyond any doubt by the most rigorous medical evidence. Thus it is dishonest to try, as the neo-conservative revisionists have tried to show with their false brownstudies, that there is something unusual or aberrational in the desire to do yard work in the nude.

In fact it is quite obvious from examining the nude yardman's life, and the growth of the nude yardworker movement in general, that there was a logical, inevitable progression of things that led up to it, as natural as the passing of the seasons.

The nude yardman grew up in a small southwestern town that was ringed by beautiful, snow-capped mountains. This was, it was said, the place where dreams came true. And come true they did for many people who moved out here from 'back East', for the skies were clear and blue, the territory vast, and the opportunities many. The people were smart, strong and good looking. Good work habits and humble living were observed and rewarded. There was none of the unwillingness to try new things that characterized living 'back East'.

On the south side of town there was plenty of crime and poverty to temper one's native enthusiasm, but on the north side of town law and order prevailed, and one could ride one's bicycle around in the neighborhood if one were a young boy without any fear of being accosted for money or sport. Or walk to school in safety. Which is what the nude yardman did on a regular basis when he was not riding his bicycle to school.

The nude yardman's name was Charles Morgan Prendergast. At six years old, he was a golden haired young boy who loved to ride his scooter around the house and knock things over, make apple juice popsicles, and play video games, pretty much what every other six year old boy likes to do.

The nude yard man's mother, Jody, was a prototypical soccer mom. She was somewhat artsy-fartsy, very touchy-feely, and aspired to be lottsy-tottsy, but somehow always fell short of that latter goal. One day she and Charles Morgan's paternal uncle, whose real name was Bartholomew, but whom everybody called 'Uncle Winkle', got into an argument, which wasn't really an argument, really, so much as a difference of opinion over the meaning of things. She claimed that she believed in *emotional intelligence*, and Bartholomew, or rather 'Uncle Winkle', had heard his brother, the nude yardman's father, use this term the week before and had cringed when he had heard him use it...now he knew where he had gotten it from!

To Uncle Winkle the term "emotional intelligence" was an abomination, an oxymoron of the highest degree. He hated it. But to Jody, it was one of her favorite terms. 'Emotional intelligence', in her mind, was a substitute for the book learning and formal education she didn't have, a far cry above street smarts or mere animal shrewdness. In other words, it was a legitimate and respectable substitute for the formal education she didn't have, and probably never would have. She had read somewhere growing up, that it was impossible to measure a person's intelligence using standardized tests, and she agreed with that, of course. But she was also quite sure that if a test was ever invented for 'emotional intelligence' she would score very high on it, perhaps even place at the top of the list. She had developed this theory to a fine art form in her mind, and could discuss it with the new people in her life, potential new acolytes, who were always interested to hear about it from her. This was her way of making up for not having a Princeton or Harvard degree, or a degree from one of those other fine universities which established a person's pedigree beyond a shadow of a doubt, even the pedigrees of those members of the graduating classes who went on to become crooked politicians, corporate lawyers, and munitions manufacturers.

To Uncle Winkle, however, the term was an abomination. Emotions were the exact *opposite* of the reason and rationality that Uncle Winkle supposed was the basis of intelligence. Emotions were in fact, *irrational.* How could one have 'emotional intelligence' then? It was an impossibility, a contradiction in terms. Either one was emotional, and irrational, or one was unemotional, and rational. Belief in one's own emotional intelligence (sic), led to a belief in one's own, solipsistic view of the world. It lent credence to one's crazy ideas and often-as-not wrong intuitions. It took one out of the world of reliable platonic ideals and was, therefore, to be avoided at all costs. There was of course a place for emotions in the world. Uncle Winkle did not deny that. Love and hate, happiness and sadness certainly existed in the world and were fine all by themselves. But linking emotions and reason together made him shudder with distaste. It was an example of really fuzzy thinking. His innate contempt for the fuzzy thinking and overly simplistic views of others, which had no firm grounding in reality, or so he thought, is what turned Uncle Winkle into a proud and steadfast recluse, by the way.

But despite her eccentric homegrown philosophy, which was in the final analysis completely harmless except to her brother-in-law's finely honed sense of The Way Things Should Be, Jody was a good person and an almost perfect mother for the nude yardman. She performed her marketing and household chores cheerfully, and met all Charles Morgan's needs and demands with attention and good humor. She also performed her wifely duties with enthusiasm and gusto, and genuinely, as everyone admitted, was head over heels in love with her husband Thomas.

Thomas, the nude yardman's father made his living as a real estate investor and developer. The place where dreams came true was growing rapidly. Everybody wanted to move there, or so it seemed. The city was the home of a popular and well-loved 'party-school' university that was at the top of its collegiate league in baseball, football and many other competitive athletic pursuits. Since the sun shone 90% of the time and the weather was almost always beautiful, how could you not love to practice your sport? And thus, how could you not rise to the top of your league? The climate also attracted a huge number of earnest young people eager to learn, and a large, learned faculty. This mecca of pleasurable learning, besides attracting a huge annual influx of pilgrims eager to learn, also attracted a huge number of adjunct hangers-on. Cooks, tavern owners, bicycle shop proprietors, car mechanics, etc. They all needed places to live and places to conduct business. Furthermore, of the many men and women who attended the university from afar, many of them either stayed outright after they finished their degree, or perhaps they never finished their schooling and stayed in town to become programmers, designers, taxi drivers, salesmen, or what have you, simply because they liked the area. So there was a constant increase in the population, a population which needed roads, schools, hospitals, golf courses, office buildings, and houses.

All of those things needed land to build on. Fortunately or unfortunately, there was only so much of it to go around. During the time the nude yardman's father lived there, you could spit on the ground anywhere in or around the outskirts of the growing city and know that where the spit landed would be a good place to buy land to make money on. A twelve-year-old could spit on land and make money buying and selling real estate in that town at that time.

But Thomas wasn't a 12 year old boy. He had a much keener mind than that. He wasn't originally from the place where dreams come true, he had gone to the university on a baseball scholarship. He had been a star pitcher at an exclusive boarding school back East and had gone out to The "U", as it was called sometimes, because it was the 'Number 1' college in the country as far as baseball went. His plan was to become a pitcher for a Major League team, either the Detroit Tigers or the Boston Red Sox if he had his way, and so he figured on playing four years of college ball and then going into the majors. And what better place to do that then at the Number 1 baseball school in the country? He had passed the try-outs with flying colors. Out of the 150 freshmen who had tried out and wanted to pitch, he had been selected for the pitching squad, along with 3 others. But then the coach called him into his office one day after practice and broke some bad news to him. Routine x-rays had revealed that his ankles were weak. He might be rounding second base one day and they might go out on him, so they said. The team doctors, who were paid to decide on such things, couldn't say when it would happen, but they said it definitely would happen. They were employed by the Number 1 collegiate team in the nation to pontificate on such matters and so their word was law. It wouldn't be fair to him (Thomas) or the team to let him play anymore. Even though Thomas got down on his hands and knees and begged the coach to let him stay on the team, because all he had ever wanted to do ever since he was little was to play baseball, and he promised to sign any insurance release the coach wanted him to sign, the coach refused to relent. "Sorry, I can't let you play, son! It wouldn't be fair to you or the team. But good luck to you! And don't forget to clean out your locker before you leave!"

So after a few more semesters, frustrated by his inability to play baseball, Thomas had quit school and had gone into real estate and had made a fortune doing so. It was a consolation prize of sorts for not being able to play baseball. Over the years he was able to provide for his wife and young son who soon came along, and had bought a big house over on the northeast side of town. There they lived in style and comfort as Charles Morgan was growing up. After a while, Thomas convinced his mother and brother to move out to join him in the place where dreams came true. After visiting the town a few times, and liking it, they both agreed to do so. Eventually they moved into the same neighborhood where Thomas lived so that the family could get together often for birthdays and special occasions without having to travel far. In fact, they were all within walking distance of each other, which is a nice thing for a family.

Besides his penchant for nude yardwork, the nude yardman lived a fairly normal childhood. One of the nude yardman's best friends in his childhood years was Mary Ashley. He met Mary in a Waldorf School where they shared a big box of Crayola Crayons together because the school was not rich enough to buy everyone a big box of Crayola Crayons with all the cool, offbeat colors that spiced up childhood drawings. They drew UFO's and aliens, and houses, and birds, and dragons and castles, and fair maidens, and jousting knights, and other things from real life and fairy tales. Their crayon drawings remained stuck on each of their family's refrigerators with magnets for months on end and made their parents beam almost endlessly when they looked at them.

Mary's favorite color to use was coral pink, and his was royal purple, so that their drawings tended to have a lot of these two colors in them. But they were not averse to using other colors, too. And lest anyone steal one of the 152 colors that they had available from their box, they guarded it jealously, and were careful to see that it was always properly put away each time they used it with all the colors intact. Mary was a very good friend, and considering that they never lost a color together, a pretty reliable one, too. They had never gotten around to kissing each other because each was a little too young to think of that then. But don't you worry, they got around to it later!

2

Uncle Winkle and the Oracle

Charles Morgan's uncle Winkle was the original nude yard-man, at least in a way. Charles Morgan had seen him watering his petunias one day in the buff and had liked the way Uncle Winkle looked, the graceful way the hollows in the outsides of his buttocks opened and closed when he walked, how supple his thigh muscles were when the flexed, and how his chest and ribs stood slightly puffed out like a hairy bird's when he stood erect. He looked like Michelangelo's *David*. Charles Morgan was too young to recognize him as such, having never even heard of the Renaissance sculptor before when he first saw him like that, but if he had heard of him, he would have recognized him as look-ing like a Michelangelo sculpture immediately. Bartholomew did not mean to become an example for his nephew. It was just an accident that happened. One morning when his nephew was visiting before he had put his clothes on, he was strolling in his walled-in backyard and had noticed that his flowers needed watering. So he had put his coffee cup down and gotten the hose and started watering them. That was how it happened.

Uncle Winkle called Charles Morgan "the little wiggle worm" because when he used to spend the night and sleep with him he would wiggle one way and then the other before he would fall asleep. Charles Morgan, after he heard this word enough, then began to call his uncle "Uncle Winkle" slurring over the gg's the way a young child would. That's where the nickname came from. And you know how nicknames get started from the smallest, illogical trifle and somehow persist.

Uncle Winkle was Charles Morgan's lifelong best friend, and tutor in math and science. He had advanced degrees in almost every subject you could think of, and was generally known around town as a walking encyclopedia. Uncle Winkle was also a worry wart. He worried about everything. He wasn't quite to the point where he would worry while making love that the telephone might ring, but he was almost to that point. Sickening. The amount of daily worrying that he did about things, even things he didn't have any control over, like the national debt, or women's use of high heels, was sickening, and he knew it was a problem, or at least admitted it was to himself privately sometimes when it seemed like it might be especially out of control. He wished there was somebody he could talk to about this, but he didn't trust psychiatrists. As a class, they were almost worse than personal injury lawyers. The idea that you could lay bare your soul to a perfect stranger, who could then by knowing your mind, have almost complete control over you, was anathema to Uncle Winkle; especially when that control allowed them to indulge their pet, seemingly-well-intentioned theories of important mental processes, or their vested commercial interests of finding heretofore unknown problems with you and your psyche, and extending your 'visits' for treatment at rates which made the rates of emergency house-call plumbers seem reasonable. It was clearly unethical for a licensed health care professional to do things like that, and not all of them did. But Uncle Winkle knew that enough of them did do it so that it was best to be wary of them. Several years ago a female psychiatrist had been hacked to death by a former patient with a meat cleaver, and Uncle Winkle had followed the case in the newspapers. While he felt sympathy for the woman, he could almost understand the motivations of the former patient. "Leave me alone! Will you?" he imagined the patient saying. And when the doctor had not left him alone, but had continued to play with his over-stressed and delicate mind, he had snapped.

"Do you get teased a lot about your Uncle Winkle?" The school children would ask Charles Morgan.

"Yeah, of course. What do you think? He's normal?" Charles Morgan would answer. The relationship between them was a unique and curious one. Charles Morgan absorbed as much as he could about incomplete sets, and combinatorial mathematics, and Calabi-Yau manifolds that Uncle Winkle tried to teach him, trying to make his Uncle Winkle feel better by letting him teach him about those subjects, and being as respectful as he could toward him, but all the while harboring secret doubts about the practical utility of such things. This despite revered feelings regarding the sacred power and majesty of such intricate inventions of the human mind.

Among other things, Uncle Winkle was a blue blocker sunglasses nut. He hadn't believed that they would work at first. He had seen the television commercials, and had scoffed at the notion that a pair of sunglasses could change your life. But then he had come across a pair half-buried in the sand at the beach that somebody had forgotten, and he had tried them on, and...voila!

Whereas before his appearance had been rather humdrum and grey, now with his blueblockers on, he looked like a Hollywood mogul or famous actor trying to remain anonymous; so that when he went into the *Shop and Go!* supermarket where he liked to go to shop and sometimes watch the lobsters in the tank, people would whisper over in the fruit juice aisle, "Who is that guy?" and he would pretend not to notice. Not that he wore them for that! Oh no, he wore them for the mystical, magical effect they had on his visual field. They literally took him into a different world when he put them on, a world that was cleaner, brighter and more colorful. A world that appeared to have been painted by an artist with a fuller, more extensive palette. Or it was as if the ordinary visual world was an overexposed photograph, with all the colors bleached out, whereas with his blueblockers on, the exposure level was perfect.

He couldn't believe it when he first put them on, and was in his own private world of ecstasy for days looking at things. The birch trees glowed whiter, the autumn foliage was crisper and brighter. The puffy, white cumulus clouds, which looked pretty good anyway, looked more lovely. It was a visual feast.

Everything in the ordinary world turned into eye candy. It was like having the visuals of an acid trip without having to take the acid.

At first people thought Uncle Winkle had developed a new type of epileptic palsy which might be of interest to medical authorities when he first discovered the blueblockers because he couldn't stop looking at things in a preternaturally-fixed, almost catatonic sort of way when he had them on. In fact, when he was wearing the blueblockers he appeared to be somewhere far off in space, even during the most routine, everyday chores such as trips to the grocery store or driving his nephew back from school. Sometimes his relatives would try to establish contact with him during these moments of apparent absence. "Earth to Uncle Winkle," they would say, passing their hand in front of his eyes, trying hard to register some emotion on his face. But there never was any. During such moments, Uncle Winkle was simply transfixed by the beauty of the natural world which existed all around him, a beauty which somehow escaped ordinary perception before but which somehow using the magical gateway of the blueblockers' special spectrum adjustment, he was able to behold. During such transcendental moments, Uncle Winkle really was lost in his own world, like an autistic child, and it seemed like nothing could bring him back. But just when his friends and relatives had given up all hope that Uncle Winkle had not actually turned into a vegetable, or that the car that was careening toward them was not actually going to hit them and kill everybody inside, that Uncle Winkle would snap back to his normal self and avert the incipient catastrophe.

Luckily, this period of deeply altered consciousness, brought about by the chance discovery of a pair of blueblocker sunglasses on the beach, during which time people wondered with a good bit more than their usual vigor whether or not Uncle Winkle was indeed going to be led off by the little men in white coats, lasted only a few weeks. But afterwards, Uncle Winkle didn't just stay immersed in his own world after discovering the new, wonderful visual panoramas available with the blueblockers. He became positively evangelical about them, inviting everybody he met, even strangers that he met occasionally and had a conversation with when he had them on, to try them out. "Here, try these! You'll love 'em" he'd say, and the other party, maybe an Uber driver who was giving him a ride or a person he had asked directions of, would try them on and agree with Uncle Winkle that indeed they were great and had a super-special effect on their vision, bobbing their heads up and down with enthusiasm in agreement, although exactly how many people actually went out and bought themselves a pair as a result of Uncle Winkle's benevolent influence was never determined by anything resembling careful statistics.

Getting in a groove, that was what Uncle Winkle called it. Getting in a groove, to drive, to ski, to chop wood, to do good outdoor work of any kind. In order to get in the groove, even for just simple, ordinary living, on a day-to-day level, Uncle Winkle felt it was necessary to have one's blueblockers on. So that if one were driving to the grocery store, one needed them on. Or if one was driving cross country, perhaps to visit an old friend, one needed them on. To take a walk in the woods, one needed them on. To take a stroll by the sea, one needed them on. To take a boat ride, one needed them on. To go to one's nephew's baseball game, one needed them on. If one did not have them on, if perhaps one forgot them in a haste to leave the house, where, thank God, Uncle Winkle did *not* wear them (a fact which was avidly discussed by his closest relatives when the troublesome but somehow always curiously welcome subject of Uncle Winkle came up) it was an unforgivable sin. In his opinion, Hollywood had gotten it all wrong with its long list of characters who wore sunglasses, like Jack Nicholson, Brad Pitt and Angelina Jolie. Sunglasses were not important for how you *looked* with them on, but for how you could *look* with them on. If they were the right pair, and properly cleaned, they could return one to that perfect state of childhood innocence, giving one an inner sense of peace and serenity that transcended the fraught moments of the day. In view of all the frenzy and anxiety which went on in modern day life, they were extremely important.

Besides wearing blueblocker sunglasses, Uncle Winkle occasionally liked to go to the supermarket and watch the lobsters. They were in a big glass aquarium tank in the seafood section back near the deli and day-old fruits and vegetables. Generally there were about twenty or thirty of them in the tank.

Uncle Winkle marveled at how much care the store's lobsters received. The front of their glass tank was always clean and the water in their tank was always crystal clear. It must have cost the supermarket a fortune to keep all those lobsters so well cared for in there, thought Uncle Winkle. They were being kept alive and on display, of course, for the purpose of being purchased by the discerning public, the idea of so transparent a display of such living creatures being for the sensible reason that if a customer was somewhat picky about their choice of lobster, and wanted an especially healthy and clean-looking one, they could point through the glass to a particular lobster and say, "There, I want that one!" and expect that the girl behind the counter, leaning over to try and see better, would know which one they meant.

The side benefit of keeping these denizens of the deep alive with a clear glass partition between their world and the busy supermarket world of humans instead of frozen on ice, was that you could watch them and if you were really, *really* careful, notice that they were watching you, too. That was what Uncle Winkle found so fascinating. Here was an actually observant, intelligent species, he thought the first time he made the discovery that the lobsters were watching him with the same apparent interest that he was watching them with.

In order to get inside their heads to understand what thoughts might be running through their heads when they were watching him, Uncle Winkle tried imagining that he shared their plight, that he was a lobster in that tank with his claws kept tightly shut by a thick rubber band.

Well, didn't he sometimes feel like his strong, 'invincible' claws were banded shut by the powers that be? Didn't he have issues with the forces of orthodoxy, establishment and tradition that made him frustrated and angry? Didn't he have well-meant, inchoate designs to take over the reigns of government, let all the innocent prisoners free, and declare a brave new world, where the strong and good and innocent ruled, and the evil, greedy bastards who were running the show now all went to jail; and in all other ways right all the wrongs that the current establishment had given their blessing to? Of course he did! But in so many ways his monumental strivings, his hopes and his dreams were stymied. So he could only sympathize with the lobsters cooped up in the tank who he imagined might be thinking that if they could only wield their mighty claws without restriction, when that grocery store seafood worker reached her hand into the tank to pull them out for some nobody customer with a few extra bucks in his or her pocket, they would nip a finger off, or at least cling on so hard that the store would have to call 911 and get an emergency crew with a $50,000 "jaws of life" machine to get him off!!! Oh yes, to be a lobster in that tank with one's claws free might not be so bad. But with them banded! Ah, it would be intolerable and unpleasant in the extreme! Especially given the freedom that they had had in their own realm on the bottom of the sea, where they often got together in social groups and made journeys of dozens, even hundreds of miles on strange lobster business, and did other things that seemed downright "civilized". It was no wonder PETA was so concerned about the plight of lobsters. Their situation was so patently unfair!

So by virtue of what amounted to a longitudinal study, his astute observations, and clinical patience, Uncle Winkle thought he had found a kind of doorway into the inner workings of the insect-like mind of these trapped arthropods, by cataloging their facial expressions and what seemed to be their associated emotions.[1].

The three emotions were these: Absolutely fierce ferociousness and pissed off anger, a listless passivity (pathetic surrender), and lastly, of all things, curiosity.

How exactly could you detect these emotions? It was hard to say for sure. It was very subtle. Part of it was in the way they moved and acted. The ferocious individuals were generally all by themselves, or at least by themselves as much as they could be in such a small tank. They carved out a small patch of territory for themselves and they looked liked they were ready to defend it at all costs. What were they angry about? Were they angry at the other lobsters in the tank? Perhaps. But it was also obvious, as one could tell by looking at them, that they were also angry at some of the humans who looked in at them through the glass, individuals who represented the last link in the long chain of their unaccustomed custody and their status as expensive caloric commodities, elements of a sophisticated 'food chain', instead of free-ranging creatures in control of their own destiny. Strange as it might sound, they seemed to have an inkling of this food chain (perhaps by virtue of recent contact with it?) which consisted of the many men and women of our species who had built the clever, bottom-resting traps, for these curious, backward-walking creatures to walk into, laid those traps, hauled them up into their wet, heaving boats, taken them out of the traps, banded them with elastic bands, and carried them *en masse* to the fish market to be sent hither and yon into the countryside, alive and green, before they were selected by the impatient, demanding hominids who would plunge them in boiling hot water and turn their shells angry red. These fierce, ferocious lobsters were generally found sitting on top of a pile of their comrades.

The ones who had the expressions of 'surrender' on their 'faces' were generally at the bottom of the piles of three or four lobsters that built up in corners of the tank, their bodies sprawled willy-nilly across each other in like the victims of the Nazi gas chambers trying to crawl their way upward to the last vestiges of fresh air. Uncle Winkle imagined that their heart rates and blood pressure were suppressed and that they did not have the will to live any longer. Unfortunately, they could not sleep in that tank for slight movements of the other creatures in the pile would lead to movements of the whole pile itself which would disturb their individual slumber. So, being denied sleep, which is recognized as an element of torture among the signatories to the Geneva Convention, and an obvious impediment to the health and well being of all species, the lobsters suffered mightily. The weaker ones, deprived of a proper environment in which to live, simply settled to the bottom of the tank and stayed there, pathetically resigned to their fate.

In between the hopping mad lobsters and the apathetic, resigned ones, there were the curious ones. They seemed to be in okay shape, physically, avoided both the hopping mad lobsters and the piles of the apathetic ones and kept to themselves, except every once in a while they went on a grand tour around the little confines of the tank to see what they could find. Not that they could find very much because the tank wasn't very big, but at least they tried. Uncle Winkle concluded they were capable of cognition and had a well-defined mental state, for they looked right out at you through the glass with what seemed to be detached puzzlement.

They *seemed* to be curious about three different things. One, their plight: how was it that they had ended up in that tank? Two, the brightly-lit world that existed beyond the glass walls of their container: what were all the strange things and goings-on that they saw in that air-filled world that did not look at all like the things and goings-on on the seabeds that they were accustomed to. And three, the relationship between the strange, air-filled world and their plight.

As part of their interest in the strange, air-filled world, they appeared to be very interested in the beings that inhabited that world. It seemed they could tell that sentient beings with a purpose inhabited that air-filled world. When they were being observed by someone, for instance, a young child with his or her mommy who had never seen the lobsters before and came to gaze at them for a minute or two while they did their shopping, they would look right back at that person, much as that person looked in at them, in a sort-of staring match, trying to figure out what the connection was.

It was during such moments of his own observations of these crustaceans that Uncle Winkle imagined that he had a mind to mind contact with the lobsters and conversations took place between himself and members of that species which sometimes went like this:

LOBSTER: "Why did you put me in here?"

UNCLE WINKLE: "I didn't put you in there, somebody else did."

LOBSTER: "Well, why did THEY put me in here? It's way overcrowded, there's not enough oxygen in this water, and I can never get any sleep."

UNCLE WINKLE: "To eat you."

LOBSTER: "*Eat* me?!? Why? Why would anyone want to eat *me*, for heaven's sake?"

UNCLE WINKLE:"I don't know. I guess they like the way you taste."

LOBSTER: "I taste terrible! I never asked for this. I was walking backwards, *backwards* mind you when I went into that trap. I wasn't going for the bait! It's all a horrible accident. Please let me out!"

UNCLE WINKLE: "I don't have the power to let you out. You're in a commercial establishment. It would be against the sacred profit principle for *Shop and Go!* to let you out. Why I'd be fighting the whole edifice of capitalism and the organizing structure of business practices built up over thousands of years to get you released. It could never be done. Forget it."

LOBSTER: "But you're a *scientist,* for heavens sake. You know I have *consciousness.* Here you are having a Vulcan mind meld with me, you can read my thoughts, and you've been doing it for who-knows-how-long. You know I have consciousness, and *am* sentient. So how can you let them *eat* me? Isn't it against your credo?"

UNCLE WINKLE: "Simply because I do not have the money or the resources to let you out. Let's be practical. To let you out I would have to spend approximately $1,079.10. The price the *Shop and Go!* has put on you, the ransom, so to speak, is $11.99 per pound, times an estimated 3 lbs of you, times the number of your mates in there, which is 30, for I could never rescue just one of you. I would have to rescue you all, or I wouldn't feel right. So $1,079.10 in total. $35.97 for each one of you. And I would have to do it every time a fresh batch of your chums came in on the seafood truck, for who knows how many years in order to feel right. I'm sorry to have to be the one to acquaint you with certain aspects of the Facts of Life, but throughout History, scientists have often had to hold back their misgivings and watch powerlessly as grave injustices are done simply because the more powerful forces of commercial self-interest are opposed to their ideas. What you are asking me to do is to commit economic suicide, because I only have $3,495 in the bank and I need that for all my expenses, which you will be glad to know do not include the purchase of lobsters to eat. So I am very sorry, Mr. Lobster, but according to my great mentor Socrates, it is necessary for me to love myself above all else. And if I were committing economic suicide I would not be heeding that credo. I should very much like to help you and be your white knight in shining armor, but I simply cannot."

It was during such imaginary conversations, when he sympathized with the plight of the lobsters but reminded himself that he could do nothing about it, that he usually remembered how the PETA[2] organization had, with great fanfare, some years back, bought a live lobster in a midwestern supermarket, purchased an airplane ticket for it, flown it to the coast, and then released it back into the ocean as a publicity stunt. At the time he had heard about it, he thought that it was silly. Imagine a $400 airplane ticket for a lobster! But that was before he had started making these pilgrimages to the *Shop and Go!* to observe the lobsters and began to understand them. After he started these visits and began his intricate, solitary behavioral studies, which one day someone in authority might recognize as being a great but previously undiscovered work of science on par with Darwin's *The Origin of Species*, or some other great, controversial work, and if not that great then perhaps leaning in that direction, he felt a great deal more kinship with the PETA people, and appreciated their efforts a lot more; even though he never became a member of their organization.

But even though Uncle Winkle had made the decision not to spring the lobsters with his own money, he was conflicted about that decision, because he really did want to do it. He assuaged his guilt by thinking to himself that if he ever did get rich, for instance, if he was ever bequeathed a fantastically large sum of money by a great aunt that he didn't know he had, or if he bought a lottery ticket and suddenly became a winner, or if he stumbled across a masterpiece in Goodwill and managed to buy it quite innocently for $14 and then find out it was worth $7 million a few months later, he would go out on a lobster buying spree, a real fling, and buy freedom for tankfuls and tankfuls of poor, mistreated lobsters, and set them all free. He was sure he would feel good about it. And the lobsters involved would feel good about it, too. And the lobster species would feel good about it, and the human species would feel good about it too, that is if they could be informed of the undertaking in precisely the right way. He wasn't sure exactly how many tankfuls it would take to set his mind right for all the surreptitious, dispassionate behavioral studies he had performed on them, even if such behavioural studies had been entirely imaginary and conducted entirely in his own mind and concerned abstract psychological questions of inter-species behavior, rather than dismal facts of physiology and anatomy such as what temperature their flesh froze at, but he was sure that some sort of reasonable, compromise number of tankfuls could be reached that would absolve him from all the sins he had committed while watching the lobsters over all those years and doing nothing to save them.

Why was Uncle Winkle so interested in the lobsters in the first place? The answer has many parts. In the first place, as opposed to the ground beef, tuna steaks, or the roasted chickens, or the pork chops, or the potato chips or the cubes of beef bouillon, the roll-on deodorant, or any other thing in the store, the lobsters were alive. Oh, maybe the fresh scallions had cells in them that were still alive. And sure all the other fruits and vegetables did, too. And yes, some of the *acidophilus* bacteria in the yogurt were alive. But none of the fruits and vegetables or bacteria, wholesome or otherwise, had consciousness, as far as he knew. The fact that they were alive and *conscious* set the meaty lobsters apart as a special anomaly, even in a great, far-flung emporium like the *Shop and Go!* which had so many exotic things in it like pickled pigs knuckles, canned sardines, and wheels of bleu-veined rochefort cheese. Secondly, the *Shop and Go!* in effect kept the lobsters alive as *prisoners*, and Uncle Winkle, ever since he had read those World War II POW escape stories about Colditz Castle, the stories about the concentration camps, Solzhenitsyn's *The Gulag Archipelago*, Foucault's *Discipline and Punishment, Panopticon*, and a few other books in that genre, was interested in prisoner populations as a sort of hobby. A lot of people share that same interest, believe it or not. Thirdly, the lobsters in the tank were denizens of a completely self-contained world, a *microcosm*. Microcosms were one of Uncle Winkle's special interests. These little self-contained worlds like the stolen galaxy that hung from the cat's neck in *Men in Black,* or the little worlds that were encapsulated in liquid snow globe dioramas fascinated him.

Lastly, but perhaps not least important, as a species, the lobsters were so very *different* from human beings. They were so *alien-like* in their physiognomy, that Uncle Winkle felt that they bore watching. "They bear watching," he would say to himself.

For instance, why it was that alien species from outer space who had it in for humans, and who wanted to eat or subjugate them when they invaded, were always portrayed in the movies and literature as having pronounced exoskeletons, clicking mandibles, eyestalks, and antennae, all of which the lobsters had in abundance? This question nagged at him from time to time but he could not answer it. Naturally he felt that the answer was important, so he paid extra special attention to it in his research, thinking that perhaps it held some great, redeeming merit that even he, as involved as he was in it, might not fully understand. Who knew if someday, perhaps in the far future, some chance genetic mutation might not produce a super-intelligent breed of lobster, much smarter than they were today, that would want to seek revenge on human beings for all the torture, killing, and abuse they had suffered over the years? This was so even though for the most part he was sympathetic to their plight and felt sorry for them, for, truth be known, in his heart of hearts, he felt that his imaginings that they might one day evolve into a super-intelligent race and be able to get revenge on the human race were probably pretty far-fetched. No, the lobsters were never going to rise up Planet of the Apes-like and become the dominant life form on this planet. They were always going to be caught walking backwards into small, partly dilapidated wooden traps, and be wolfed down with corn on the cob and hot butter on Fourth of July picnics.

But still the evil alien predator quality of the lobsters fascinated and sometimes worried him. And what message were human beings sending to the rest of the Universe by eating these ugly, alien-looking creatures anyway?

Looking at the lobsters wasn't the only thing Uncle Winkle liked to do at the *Shop and Go!* He liked to cruise the aisles and look at the inventory items on the shelves. He was interested in everything on them. Each aisle was like a different country, a different adventure. At either end of the store, front or back, he would walk slowly past the heads of each aisle and look down it to see what kind of adventure it held to see whether he wanted to venture down it at that particular moment on that particular day. This pattern of this looking for adventure in the aisles was never quite the same. Some days he was bored by what he found in an aisle, and on other days what he found would get him excited. Like normally he couldn't care a wit about what the women's hygiene section of the medicine/household goods/hair care products aisle had in it, but one day, quite by chance, he found himself marveling at the sheer number of different sizes and shapes and configurations of the feminine hygiene pads that the *Shop and Go!* stocked. It was almost surreal. Were today's women really that picky? Were they all really that differently shaped? Uncle Winkle wondered, if he were a woman, would there be a brand and design that he would prefer above all others? Would the color be that important to him? Coming to the end of that section he found... the condoms! A whole meter and a half by meter and a half of them! Whew! What a lot of different sizes and shapes they came in, too! And look at that per unit pricing! $166 per carton for the special, female-pleasing variety. Why that must be the most expensive per unit price in the whole store!

Uncle Winkle was enveloped in a vague but appealing feeling of safety and security when he was in the *Shop and Go!* It was a little sanctuary apart from what seemed like a mad and dangerous world outside its walls. An oasis. The clean, brightly lit aisles and the well stocked shelves filled with various human necessities with their well-thought-out prices inspired confidence in the intelligent order of the Universe. It seemed like everyone who was there among those well-stocked, brightly decorated aisles was doing what there were supposed to be doing: the stock boys filling up the shelves, the customers shopping for breakfast, lunch or dinner for themselves or for their families, management overseeing it all... and Uncle Winkle...well, Uncle Winkle... observing it all! He was like a proud plantation owner surveying his fields and his crews at work in them.

According to his way of thinking, he might be the most loyal customer of that particular *Shop and Go!,* and in the same way that familiarity with a person might lead to a certain proprietary aspect within the soul of a beloved, Uncle Winkle felt the store to be part of his own special realm.

Because he felt safe there he spent a lot of time there and because he spent a lot of time there he felt safe there. Was that a tautology? Maybe! His placid existence in the supermarket watching the lobsters, shopping for groceries, talking to his friends, and finely observing the various scenes of purposeful human behavior completed a virtuous circle which really helped Uncle Winkle properly cope with the stress he felt from modern life. Uncle Winkle had discovered an interesting truism of modern life: if you want to calm yourself down, take a trip to the supermarket! (Yes, shopping therapy is real! Try it sometime!)

He thought it was very interesting, from a psychological point of view how perfect strangers could come together so peacefully inside a supermarket and all get along. Doubtless other people thought a lot about the supermarkets where they shopped, how they compared with others in the same neighborhood or across town, for instance, but Uncle Winkle thought about his *Shop and Go!* far more than the average citizen thought about the supermarket where they shopped, and perhaps more than any other person in History thought about the supermarket where they shopped (but of course it would be hard to design a protocol to test this conjecture so we must leave it to the realm of speculation for the time being). Anyway, we know that the average person certainly spends a lot of time thinking about the supermarket where they shop simply because groceries are such an important thing in their lives.

It was Uncle Winkle's close association with the Oracle that had given him his almost supernatural ability to understand the thoughts of the lobsters for the Oracle had the ability to see into the lives of others and to understand them, and had shown him how to do it, too. She could simply say, on a fine Spring morning, sitting on a bench with Uncle Winkle, suddenly dropping everything else, "Listen! Hear the robins? They are arguing over where to build their nest!" And with just those few words, she could impart the miraculous, uncanny ability to interpret the speech of robins to Uncle Winkle so that for all that morning Uncle Winkle felt he could understand what the robins were saying as clearly as if they were speaking the Queen's English.

That was the power that the Oracle had. By just being around her you could do wonderful things that you didn't ordinarily have the power to do, even though after you left her, that ability would fade and you would slowly become normal again as her spell dissolved (leading one to the conclusion that proximity to her was a very desirable thing!)

The Oracle, whose real name was Persephone Adams, lived in a small *casita* all by herself, with scores of plants of all kinds which she talked to, cared for, and treated like friends. She had one black and white cat named Steinway, named for the maker of pianos. He was a loyal companion, and a very smart cat. He had just showed up one day, walked in the door of the *casita* and decided to stay. It was said that Steinway "adopted" the Oracle, rather than the other way around.

The Oracle was Uncle Winkle's best friend and lover. She tolerated all his eccentricities and didn't demand much of him except that he do what he said he was going to do, and make plans that he followed through on. If he didn't show up when he said he was going to and didn't call to tell her why, boy was he in trouble.

The Oracle was the most beautiful woman in the town. And the most intelligent. Everybody knew that. She was head and shoulders smarter than everybody, including Uncle Winkle. And she had lots of friends because they all wanted her opinion on things that they needed help figuring out. The Oracle would have them over for tea, or lunch, or supper, or perhaps even for breakfast sometimes, listen to them, and then tell them what she thought and how they should proceed to get the best results.

And she was almost always right, which is why she had a lot of friends.

When Uncle Winkle came over they would play chess together. When she first met Uncle Winkle she didn't play chess. Uncle Winkle would spot her a rook, two bishops, and a queen and still win. But because she knew Uncle Winkle liked to play chess she had arranged to take lessons from a grandmaster in town, and had learned to play, so she could offer him a better game. She had learned to play so well that she could now beat Uncle Winkle 2 times out of 3. That was how much she loved him. She went out of her way to learn a game that he loved just to please him. Besides playing chess, they went hiking together, traveled to distant lands together, solved crossword puzzles together, invested in stocks and bonds together, and talked about everything under the Sun together, agreeing on most things, but not everything, obviously.

One day Uncle Winkle brought his nephew over and left him with The Oracle for a few hours because he had some business in town. She was glad to help 'babysit'. When he came back to pick him up, The Oracle praised young Charles Morgan. She said, "He likes to clean, and pickup, and put things where they belong. He's a good worker."

3

───

The Nude Yardman's Father Gets Arrested

As a mark of his almost legendary self-discipline, Tom, the nude yard man's father, rose every morning at 5:30 am and took the family dog on a walk. It was something he had been doing since before he got married. Sometimes he met his friend, a retired army colonel, on the outskirts of a nearby golf course that was deserted at that hour, and they would walk their dogs together, mostly silently, because nobody has much to say that early in the morning, but sometimes also with the usual amount of good conversation that can be expected from close friends. Or he would take the walk alone with the dog on his own property and occasionally throw a stick for him to retrieve. One fine morning, in early February, he rose to take the dog on his daily constitutional and heard an enormous, thundering din coming from near the front of the house. "Oh my," thought Tom. "What could that be?" He went around to the front of the house to see an armored car and 50 black jacketed SWAT assault team members crashing through his front gate, streaming towards his house.

"What the heck?" he thought.

You see, besides making his living as a real estate investor, the nude yard man's father also had an "extra-curricular" activity. He was tangentially involved, mostly for the thrill that clandestine activities bring, and on an occasional basis only, of helping to connect people who wanted to be connected. These people who wanted to be connected did what might be called the quintessential American avocation of the late twentieth century: they traded in a certain species of dried flowers that were actually a banned horticultural product, i.e., *cannabis sativa.* [3]

While he was in college, Tom had met and made friends with several individuals who were from Mexico. Their families owned farms where thousands of acres of luscious, fragrant cannabis grew, ten, twelve, fifteen feet high. Over the years, Tom had connected people, friends of friends, from all over the United States with his other friends in Mexico who he had met in college And the authorities were finally coming for him because of the role he had played in connecting the various parties. Helping people ship tractor trailer loads of good, fresh bud up North? Well, you couldn't say it wasn't fun while it lasted!

They came storming at him in their black uniforms like angry bats out of hell.

His dog had just had a fresh litter of puppies who were with him on the patio. "I got puppies!" he yelled, sensing an imminent danger to them and hoping to alert his attackers that innocents were in harm's way. "We don't give a damn about your fucking puppies," one of them growled. Two red laser spots lit up his forehead. "Down on the ground, muther-fucker!" one of them said. The other said, "If you move, we'll kill you." What was he supposed to do, move to get down on the ground....or stay still? Now there was a conundrum! They grabbed him and threw him on the ground while he was still deciding. Both his wife and son were watching through the glass doors on the patio in their pajamas. They had heard the commotion and had rushed over to the sliding glass door to see what was going on.

Ouch! What a nightmare. Clearly the worst day of his life. The senior agents in charge from all the relevant federal and state authorities came strutting in like peacocks after it was clear the danger was over. Friendly fire episodes were notorious in those early morning busts when everybody was pumped up on Red Bull and steroids and hadn't gotten a normal night's sleep. And they didn't want to become a statistic. They put Jody and Charles Morgan in one of the assault vehicles and locked them in. Then they came over to Tom and wanted to know where all the money was hidden. "What money?" Tom asked. "The millions of dollars in cash we know you have hidden on this property." Tom laughed. "There are not millions of dollars in cash hidden on this property. What are you, kidding?"

Well, that is something he might have said anyway, even if there *was* a hidden cache of money someplace on the property, right? I mean, some people would say that. But in fact there wasn't one. You see, Tom did not make much money from putting people on one side of the border in touch with other people on the other side of the border. He just did it mostly because it was exciting and he was trying to help The Cause. You know what 'Cause' I am talking about, right? The *Cause* of the True Believer. Oh the parties he connected threw him a bone every once in a while. But mostly they did not. So there wasn't a large cache of illegally obtained U.S. currency hidden somewhere on his property, even though the federal agents wanted there to be one. In fact there wasn't a large cache of illegally obtained U.S. currency anywhere, except in the Swiss bank account of the guy who had finked on Tom because, after all, he wanted to keep it after he had been caught, and by ratting on Tom he knew he would be allowed to.

Truth be known, if they had simply served Tom with an arrest warrant he would have appeared in court when they wanted him to without all the fuss. But the law enforcement personnel who mounted the raid who claimed they were trying to eliminate the threat of addictive drugs were in fact all addicts themselves, of adrenaline. They loved the soaring adrenaline rush of the early morning military-style attacks on the civilians accused of violations of the drug laws. They were almost without exception persons of low self esteem so the opportunity to strut around in their flak jackets and helmets and belts filled with stun grenades with their high-powered weapons was a real ego boost. For a few moments every week they could feel important, and the rest of the time, they could think about those moments and feel important anyway! And so they served the arrest warrants this way, rather than just sending them out in the mail.

After searching the place for four hours and finding absolutely nothing, no evidence of criminal wrongdoing at all, not even an overdue library book, despite turning everything in the house upside down and inside out twice, they released Charles Morgan and Jody from the armored assault vehicle and trundled Tom off to the federal lockup in handcuffs for an arraignment to be held the following week (after he had been further interrogated and reminded several times it would be best to tell the sometimes suspiciously friendly federal agents where the large stash of illegally obtained U.S. currency was). After they left, Jody and Charles Morgan wandered around the house in a daze looking at the mess the agents had made of everything. It was as if a tornado had rampaged through the house, overturning everything and destroying the peace, serenity and sense of order that had always been there before. Charles Morgan began to cry. Jody, his mom, hugged him to her bosom. "There, there" she said. "Everything will be all right. Don't cry."

The government was so convinced that Tom was an important cog in the wheel of a major international drug smuggling conspiracy thanks to the sworn affidavit of the fink (which in fact was almost completely perjurious) that they wouldn't even grant him bail. The Bail Reform Act of 1984 (notice that year) was cited. Tom, they said, posed a danger to the community. They wouldn't let him out of jail to prepare his defense. Instead they sent him to a federal detention center in a cold northern state, thousands of miles away from his home and family where many other inmates went who were awaiting trial.

It was a scary place. When you drove by it on the highway in the middle of the night all the lights were always on, blazing away all over the buildings and the exercise yards like the arc lights did at Cape Kennedy before a rocket launch, making you think that the poor fellows inside never got any rest, like those poor tortured prisoners at Guantanamo. And for the most part they didn't.

Because there was nothing in there to absorb sound, noise bounced off the hard walls and floors and ceilings inside and made the place always noisy. And it stank with an intense odor of fear and sweat that can only be described as prison odor, which results when too many men are cooped up in close proximity to each other for long periods of time against their will. There was nothing to read, nothing to do. The food was terrible and the guards mean and completely unsympathetic. It was a modern day place of crucifixion, a technological mini-hell.

I mean, imagine one day you are in the calm and loving embrace of your home and family and the next day you find yourself in a place like that. Wow! Would that make your head spin? You bet it would!

Judge Robards, the black judge who presided over the case, had been born and raised in one of that northern state's cities' poorer neighborhoods, a neighborhood that might have been called a ghetto in a previous era in American history. She was from a poor, hard-working, working class family and her family had impressed upon her conservative values and respect for the law. Many of her cohort let their poverty and their surroundings grind them down, but she refused to do so. She was determined to rise above whatever adversity life could throw at her. She became the valedictorian of her high school class, the first black girl in the history of that all-Catholic school to do so, and went on to a state university to earn her college degree. She then studied law at a law school in Boston that had a reputation for championing issues related to economic and social justice.

When she was in law school, she wanted nothing better to do than to get out and practice law and right the wrongs that had been done over time to 'her people', and we cannot fault her for wanting to. In fact it was a fairly commonplace point of view for people of her race during this time in American history to want to do the same thing. They succinctly realized that working within the power structure would yield more fruits that attempting to destroy it, a viewpoint that the violent race riots of the 1960s had helped shape. So, despite the uphill struggles involved, they became lawyers, judges and other members of the legal system. Judge Robards had been one of these stalwart individuals. After she received her law degree, she returned to her hometown in order, she thought, to make a difference. She had worked for various city departments in a legal capacity, had been a litigator in one or two private firms, and had risen up through the ranks, so to speak, of the legal system through hard work, and a devotion to the better principles of the law. It was this latter aspect that had caught the attention of the powers that be who eventually, after 20 years of watching her play by the rules and not rock the boat, had recommended her for a judgeship in the federal system.

When she had gone down to Congress for her confirmation hearing she had brought her mother and her boyfriend with her and it had been all palsy and hunk-dory with those powerful rich white Senators who saw nothing wrong with her rags to riches success story. But there was a fly in the ointment. Her home city in the cold, northern state was dying. It was dying because of the competition from foreign manufacturers and the lack of vision and integrity of the white managers who were managing the historically great fountain of industry there. Books had been written and movies made about the laziness, stupidity, cupidity, venality, and resistance to change of those white managers in the industry that was her city's major employer. In the 1950's and 1960's it was an industry that had reigned supreme in America, but as time went on, and the industry had garnered a near monopoly as a supplier to the world of a product which always seemed to be increasing in demand, they had grown fat and lazy and the well known paradigm of ego and vanity affecting decision making had taken grip, with the result that sensible, common sense decision-making was tossed out the window. Important safety data and test results were fudged. Relations with labor soured. Undeserving executives grabbed golden parachutes and multi-million dollar salaries and stock option packages and spent the day on the golf course instead of at their desks. Greed and deceit in the business became the norm. Boredom and jadedness replaced the original infectious optimism and excitement. Cities in other parts of the world began to produce what her city produced, and they were better at it. Soon people were buying the products made in these other cities and not the products made in hers. Factories were shuttered and workers laid off. Crime rose. Attitudes worsened. The local economy fell into an insurmountable and steadily worsening decline.

When she became a judge, she had to confront the fact that the city's population wanted somebody to blame for this dire situation. Eventually they conveniently decided they wanted to blame it on the recreational drug users, and the people who supplied them. Even people who had a semblance of playing a role in it were not to be spared. It was unfortunate, but for the purposes of the big picture social agenda, somebody had to be made the villain. They needed a scapegoat to direct their hate at. It soon became obvious that the good judge had to go along with the mob. Some federal judges declined to try drug cases but she was not one of them. With the fervor of a well-armored Spanish conquistador converting poor South American Indians to the Christian religion at the point of a sword (Believe in my god or die!) she threw all her weight behind the effort, and all the essence of her jurisprudence and all her fair-mindedness went out the window when it came to so-called illegal drugs. She bought hook-line-and-sinker into Nancy Reagan's anti-drug hysteria, the 'Just Say No!' Campaign taken to the nth degree that had resulted, psychologically, from a projection of Nancy's own insecurities, drug addictions, and desire to be in the lime-light (and, truth be known, a lack of anything better to do) on the docile American public. In some quarters, the idea that Nancy Reagan was really nutty, and that her ideas were laugh-able was known. But in other quarters, where people were less educated, her propaganda caught on.

The nude yardman's family waited eagerly for her ruling. Finally it came, and it was a heavy blow for Tom and his family. She gave Tom six years. In her ruling she claimed that poor Tom was *more* culpable than the other members of the alleged conspiracy. Exactly why she felt this way had to do with the fact that since Mexico had been the source of the dried flowers that had been imported to her city, and since Tom was the lowest on the map and lived the closest to Mexico (if you looked at a map of where all the various alleged perpetrators lived) he was obviously the most guilty except, of course, for the people who lived in Mexico, which to her was the ultimate source of the evil which confronted her. All of the other defendants lived to the north, geographically, of where Tom lived. Most of them lived in the same northern state where she lived. She obviously couldn't find them the most guilty since standard legal doctrine required the supplier of the banned horticultural products to be held more guilty than the consumer.

She did not examine the logical premise of this assumption in her ruling but if she had she might have wondered exactly why a supplier was held more responsible than a demander in law. Why, for instance, wasn't it just as logical for the Mexican authorities to come up to her city and haul all the flower lovers back down to Mexico for arrest, interrogation, trial, and incarceration?

In any event, even though it had been clearly established by the evidence that Tom had merely introduced the fellows who wanted to drive the dried flowers up to her northern city to an erstwhile college buddy in Mexico, who had built a half-assed tunnel to bring the dried flowers across the border, and had had a very tangential role in the whole affair, Judge Robards handed out stern justice for Tom, and by extension his family. Or should we say stern injustice, for what she handed out did not fit the traditional concept of justice as the average person conceives of it at all.

In her ruling she said that Tom had 'devastated entire neighborhoods'. But of course if she had been asked to point to exactly which neighborhoods had been devastated, she would have been hard-pressed to do so, for if she had named any particular neighborhoods, and if a fair scientific inquiry had been made of whether or not that particular neighborhood was indeed devastated by the dried flowers from Mexico that had been brought there by Tom's co-defendants, it would have been impossible to reach that conclusion with any degree of certainty, and certainly not with any degree of certainty that would carry any legal weight. In fact, if she had named a particular neighborhood it would have been possible to demonstrate the exact opposite, and therefore how flawed her ruling was, because it would have been possible to demonstrate that the neighborhood had *benefited* from their availability because they represented a healthy alternative to the much more dangerous white powder drugs that were so prevalent at the time. Furthermore, the dried flowers had demonstrated therapeutic value. So she was careful not to mention any specific neighborhood lest she get into trouble on that score, and crafted her ruling using enough vague rhetoric and platitudinous language that it would be impossible for her conclusions, which did carry legal weight, to be attacked on appeal by any lawyer clever enough to know the actual facts. This is of course what she had been trained to do in law school.

Clearly, the question that any rational person would ask is that if Tom did NOT in fact 'devastate entire neighborhoods', then why did he deserve such a harsh punishment as she handed out, a punishment that was, in comparison, as measured by the months of incarceration, in fact on par with what was received by many individuals for violent assaults and other more serious crimes?

So where did she, a federal judge charged with providing justice for society, go wrong in this decision?

In two main places. Firstly, she failed to recognize the special status of what, in Linnaeus' nomenclature, is known as *cannabis sativa*. Due to her own ignorance, both of the pharmacology and of the law, she had equated the very real dangers of the white powder drugs in her city with the imaginary, made-up, Orwellian propaganda danger of the dried flowers.

Perhaps we can understand her lack of courage in challenging the conventional wisdom of the day on this issue, the issue of the actual dangers associated with the dried flowers, given the limited amount we know about her background, even though we cannot condone it. But where she cannot be forgiven, and the second place where she went wrong, was when she turned a blind eye to the truth. She knew that the prosecutor had lied when he said he had not made any promises to Tom, tricking him into pleading guilty in exchange for a reduced sentence. She knew it deep down in her heart where people know things to be true. But still she threw the book at him. It was a choice that she later regretted when she retired from the bench and looked back at all the decisions she had made. "I wish I had the chance to do that one over again," she said to herself. "What I have learned over all these years is that the truth really does matter, more than anything else, much more than my own pet ideas about things." But it didn't matter. The damage had been done. The die had been cast. The nude yard man's father had been sentenced to a long stretch of time in federal prison unfairly, by a government he trusted, and it deeply affected the nude yard man way down in his soul, where people feel things the most.

When he went to visit his dad in the minimum security federal prison they had eventually put him in he got a stern lesson in American justice from his father. "You see what they did to me? Don't let them do that to you, Charles Morgan! Don't break the law and end up in jail like I did. I am missing some of the best years of your life growing up son, and I sincerely hope you can forgive me for it."

Now the nude yard man reacted very differently than everybody else when his father got arrested. He became very quiet. His mother was besides her self with grief and confusion, and blamed herself, too, to a certain extent, for what had happened. It was such a shock to her that she was numb with fear and anxiety and could only do what the nude yardman's father told her to do, over the prison phone once a week, otherwise she would go insane, and even so, eventually she did go insane, temporarily. It was all so sudden and bewildering, so wrong, and so worrisome. It was also so senseless and troubling, it hurt her to think about it too much. But she could not do much about it. She was powerless for the most part in dealing with the situation, except she tried to handle all her husband's affairs as best as she could with as much instruction and guidance from her husband as the intermittent prison pay phone communications between them and sporadic visits would allow.

For about a year she kept it together, with her wits about her, and managed to keep the household afloat. But then she fell in with a fast-moving crowd of party-goers from Los Angeles who loved to run white powder up their noses, "nose candy" they called it. You know the people I mean. They are in all the newspapers and magazines. And having fallen prey to that seductive lifestyle, she began to spend more and more time on the West Coast in trendy "hotspots" like Venice Beach, and Laguna Beach, away from Charles Morgan, leaving him alone in the house to fend for himself on weekends. Eventually she just didn't come home at all.

Charles Morgan had been officially abandoned according to the criteria established by the State's child welfare services department. He was in fact collateral damage of the nations controversial war on drugs. His mother had effectively lost her mind and had retreated into a fantasy world because the real world was too grim to bear. He was left to fend for himself.

So his grandmother took charge of him, driving him back and forth to school, and cooking his meals, and doing his laundry and all the other stuff that his mom used to do. And his Uncle Winkle began helping him with his homework, and practicing baseball with him, especially pitching, because by this time he was in Little League (his dad had been the coach of the team before he got arrested), and doing all the things that his dad used to do for him. But Charles Morgan had changed. He had retreated into himself like a turtle into its shell. He became apathetic, melancholy and forlorn. He lost interest in almost everything he used to like to do. Even yardwork.

At this point he didn't do yardwork in the nude anymore of course. As a wee tot, Charles Morgan had had a Garden-of-Eden-like innocence about his nude yard working activities because he was really too young to know any better. But as he grew older, and saw that everybody else kept their clothes on when they worked in the yard, he grew more and more apprehensive about doing it naked. It would be safe to call this the beginning of his cloistered, prudish phase when the forces of puritanism held sway over him as they did over everybody else. Whereas before he threw off his clothes with abandon, as he grew older, he gradually dawdled and dragged his feet about doing it, and then finally when he did do it, kept them off for shorter and shorter periods until at last, he didn't take them off at all. The power of the mob had prevailed. The tyranny of the majority had become apparent. Peer pressure, that subtle, but not-so-subtle thing, ruled his life. He had become ashamed of his nakedness. And the fact that his father had been arrested and his mother had abandoned him didn't make him feel any better about it either.

4

The Virginia Retreat

It was Uncle Winkle's friend Leigh Oilerman who got Charles Morgan to want to start doing yard work again. Leigh had made his fortune in the investment business and had retired to the countryside in Virginia near Lexington where he wrote occasional investment newsletters and gardened. He loved gardening. He was always studying books on gardening, and visiting gardens and planting new trees and shrubs and plants, and building new flowerbeds and single-handedly (that was part of the problem) making his country property into a proud emblem of his love for gardening. Truth be known, the gardening calmed him down. The years he had spent in the dog-eat-dog, shark ridden waters of American capitalism had left him slightly nervous about things, and so to prevent himself from profitlessly ruminating on those dark memories alone in his big house, he gardened, and the gardening magically took away all the worries he had. There was nothing he loved better than reaching his hands down into the moist black dirt on his Virginia farm and planting a new plant or shrub. Some he planted because he knew they would grow in the Virginia climate, and the particular combination of sun and shade that he had on his property, and some he planted as experiments. But he was always thinking about his gardens and how he could make them better. And as a result, his garden always did seem to get better.

If a particular bug or beetle appeared on the leaves of one of his broad-leafed plants, he would go to bed that night worrying about it, hoping that in the morning he would have a solution. If there had been no rain for a week or two, he would start buying the newspapers and checking the weather channel to see when he could expect rain, or whether he should start budgeting for a water truck delivery. All his energy went into gardening. It was a sort of Freudian transference of libido. Uncle Winkle, when visiting one time, had tried to get Leigh to go out one night on the town in Lexington to meet some cuties, but Leigh had declined. "I've stopped doing that, Bartholomew. And I don't miss it at all," he said. "Oh," said Uncle Winkle, disappointed that they were not going to be going into town that night so that he might bump into that buxom sweetie that had smiled at him in the bookstore that morning. It was obvious that she had more than just books on her mind!

One day, after the nude yardman's father had been arrested, and his mother had split, Uncle Winkle and Leigh Oilerman were talking on the phone. "He's awfully depressed," said Uncle Winkle about his nephew. "I wonder what will become of him. He's become listless, and lost all his drive and energy. You don't suppose that he could come out and visit you for a few weeks and help you with your gardening, do you? That would really help him. Cheer him up. Do him some good to get away from here for awhile." It was early Summer and Leigh had an awful lot of work to do on his gardens so the offer was both timely and serendipitous. "Yeah, sure. That would be fine," said Leigh, glad to help out in anyway he could. "Do I have to pay him anything?"

"Oh, no," said Uncle Winkle. "Just give him a place to stay and something to eat. And take him into town every once in a while to let him see the sights. He'll be glad to help you with your gardening. He loves gardening." And so it was settled. Uncle Winkle bought Charles Morgan an airplane ticket and cleared it with the nude yardman's mother, who after all, did call every once in a while, and off the 18 year-old went to the lovely Virginia countryside, the home of rich, successful gentleman farmers like George Washington, Thomas Jefferson and Leigh Oilerman. He would be there for three weeks to help "Uncle" Leigh. Everybody concerned thought it would be good therapy for him to get over the inexplicableness of his father's arrest, and the depression it had brought. The concrete chores of planting would help clear his mind of the weird, echoing abstractions which he could not answer, and which bothered him to the point of an incipient psychosis. Post traumatic dissociative disorder they called it.

True to the hopes and predictions of the people who loved him the most, helping Leigh with his yard work did improve the young man's outlook considerably. Unlike the once-good but corrupted wizard Saruman in Tolkien's *Lord of the Rings*, whose mind lost track of the importance of green, growing things and instead became filled with fantasies of immortality through the steel gears and cogs of his machines, Charles Morgan's mind lost almost all interest in machines and the world of machines (except for new garden tools!), and instead became focused on the concerns of the plant world, thanks to Uncle Leigh's tutelage.

One night, after their outdoor chores had been finished and they were sitting inside after dinner, enjoying each other's company, Leigh quizzed the young man about his ambitions.

"Well, young man, what do you want to do with your life, after you finish helping me with my gardening?" asked Leigh, in a fatherly tone of voice. He didn't ask such questions often, but every once in a while he did.

"I don't know," said Charles Morgan, giving the same hapless and unsatisfying answer that every young adult has always given to that question since the dawn of time. "Something good, I guess. I like music. And gardening. But I don't want to go to college."

Well, that last bit of information was interesting because he had just graduated from high school and lots of young adults are expected to go to college after they do that. In fact 66.2% of high schoolers went on to college in the year Charles Morgan graduated. So he was clearly thinking about following another path.

5

The Spiritual Transformation

His three weeks of yard work for Leigh Oilerman finished, Charles Morgan returned home to his grandmother's house considerably less morose than when he had left it. But he still suffered some pretty serious spiritual malaise. Among other things that depressed him, the scuttlebutt had it that his mom was sleeping with some random tattoo artist on Venice Beach (and was getting high and drunk all the time). And his father's legal appeal was going very, very slowly.

It was at this time that the Nude Yardman credits a nightmare for his spiritual transformation. About a week after he returned from Virginia, he was having a nightmare and the bad police were attacking his home endlessly, the way certain things seem to happen over and over again in nightmares. They were traumatizing his family for no reason, sadistically. 'No! No! No!'

he cried. 'Why don't you go away? Why do you keep on coming back again and again to hurt my daddy? He never did anything to you!"

All of a sudden a door opened in his dream, and white light pored in from the doorway, dissolving the hideous, gloating black figures of the bad SWAT team. In their place he could see a vision of himself as a little boy at his grandmothers house, helping her water the beautiful, thirsty flowers in the garden. Needless to say in this dream he didn't have any clothes on. 'Aha!' he said to himself in his dream. "Now I know what I need to do! I need to get back to my roots!" (Ahem! Notice the garden metaphor? Well that's taken straight from his written memoirs. I'm certainly not clever enough to have thought of it.)

It was then that knew he had found a way to get rid of his anguish forever.

When he woke up, he went over to his friend Mary's house. Her parents were away for the weekend. Mary was an avid gardener and especially loved citrus trees. She had a lot of them out in the backyard. "Mary, let's do some gardening," he said with an unusual amount of enthusiasm. So they went out to the garden and for the first time in many, many years, he took off all his clothes. Mary was looking in the other direction connecting up the garden hose, so that when she turned around, Charles Morgan was kneeling naked on the dirt using a claw tool to loosen up the hard ground around one of the trees so that it would absorb more water.

"Charles Morgan, what are you doing?" asked Mary.

"I'm gardening, Mary."

Yeah, but you don't have any clothes on," Mary blurted out.

"I know. It makes me feel better this way," he replied, whistling a happy little tune, glad that he had finally found the courage to do what he had really wanted to do subconsciously for a long time.

"It does?" Mary asked, dumbfounded. Then she shrugged. "Okay. Let me try it." So she took off all her clothes, too. Then she knelt down on the grass and started digging up the hard dirt like Charles Morgan did to make space for a new tree she had bought at the nursery the day before. Her breasts happily swayed merrily back and forth as she worked.

"Hey, you're right! This does feel better."

Charles Morgan explained to her about the dream, and how he had always done yard work in the nude when he was little, and how he knew somehow that if he went back to doing it, everything was going to be okay, not just for him but for everybody else, too. And, he said, because he was actually doing what he had dreamed of doing, he wouldn't have nightmares anymore. They spent the rest of the morning in blissful gardening, and then ended up making love for the first time together. 'Oh, it is sweet, sweet, sweet to follow your dreams!' they both thought before falling asleep in each other's arms, happy that they had finally consummated the love that they had felt for each other for so many years. Several days later, as a result of all the attention they received, the orange and grapefruit trees healed themselves of the diseases they had been suffering and blossomed with extraordinary exuberance. Mary and Charles Morgan stood next to the trees, looking at the soft white petals of the flowers, and breathed in the clean, heady aroma of the blossoming white citrus flowers. They both knew then that they were on to something *really* good.

"Hey this gardening in the nude is some kind of powerful magic, CM," said Mary to her best friend and now lover, Charles Morgan, who she called "CM" sometimes in a kind of friendly, way.

"I know. It's what I have to do, Mary," said Charles Morgan *uber* seriously.

She looked at him thoughtfully, suddenly worried about where it was all going to lead. People didn't ordinarily garden in the nude. Did they? Would other people understand? And what would happen if they didn't understand? And, more importantly, *what would happen to Charles Morgan if they didn't?* She felt a sudden pang of anxiety in the pit of her stomach as her mind raced to answer these difficult questions, questions that she somehow knew would come up again and again before she and Charles Morgan would ever be able to settle down and lead a normal life together.

She didn't know how right she was, as we shall see. But now we must turn our attention elsewhere.

6

The Bad President Confronts a Situation

"Yahoo!" yelled the Bad President riding his daughter's favorite rocking horse back and forth and waving his ten-gallon Texas cowboy hat in the air. His daughter, who was sitting on the carpet watching, giggled and smiled. "Whoa, Trigger! Whoa!" he said. He pretended to calm the horse down, leading it down from a gallop to a slow walk. In a *basso profoundo*, mock-Texas-Cowboy tone of voice he said: "Let's go down to the creek and see if we can pick up the trail of those rustlers who stole our cattle last night. This way," he said, turning the painted wooden horse toward his daughter.

"You didn't know your daddy could ride a horse, did you pumpkin," he said to his daughter, in his own voice. She squealed with delight and clapped her hands. "My turn, daddy.

My turn." Just at that moment, the door to the Roosevelt Room opened and the President's Chief of Staff walked in.

"Mr. President," he said, being careful to address the president in a proper, respectful manner.

"Just a second, Wendell. Can't you see I'm busy?" The President was deep into playing 'Let's Pretend' with his daughter. The *basso profoundo* voice came back and now they were down by the creek looking for the tracks of the desperadoes who had rustled their cattle in the soft beach sand. Soon darkness would fall and tracking would get more difficult. Would that mean that the no-good rustlers would be able to get away to the south, across the Rio Grande? Or would they be able to catch them?

Somewhat embarrassed by his own presence, the Chief of staff looked down at his wingtips which had been shined earlier that morning by the soft buff wheel of the automatic shoe shine machine he had ordered out of one of those expensive novelty gadgets catalogs. After it had arrived, he had placed it near the water cooler in the hallway and afterwards everybody in the White House always had shiny shoes. The Chief of Staff was very proud of that initiative of his, which had boosted morale considerably in the White House. It was one of the things he liked to ruminate on when he didn't have anything else to do. So he ruminated on how good it was for everybody to have shiny shoes in the White House, looking at his own shiny wingtips, while he waited for the President to stop playing "Let's Pretend!"with his daughter. But after a while, he felt he had to interrupt For The Good of the Nation (that was after all what he was being paid for). He cleared his throat. "Ahem," he said.

"Mr. President, I hate to interrupt, but we have...." ...dare he say it?.. " a *situation*."

"Well, of course we have a *situation*. We always have a *situation*...that's what we have the *Situation* Room for. To handle the *situation*." The President chuckled and went right on playing with his daughter.

The Chief of Staff decided to get right to the point. "Mr. President, one of our nukular bombers is missing." Like everybody else around the President, the Chief of Staff pronounced 'nuclear' 'nukular' the way the President did because they did not consider it good form or very sporting to remind the Commander in Chief of his mis-pronunciations.

This nature of this news did not seem to bother the President, either. He continued playing with his daughter, slowing easing his horse down the soft sand beach, looking down for the no good rustlers' tracks, which had to be there so they could follow them and get them before they got across the Rio Grande.

"Mr. President, not only is one of our nukular bombers missing, *but the press knows about it!*' said the Chief of Staff, a bit more anxiously.

The President blanched. The press! Why those dastardly fellows! They were really mean! They poked their noses into things where they didn't belong. And they might try to hurt him with news like that. Here was a problem that might require his attention after all!

"Daddy has to go back to work now, pumpkin," he said getting off the horse "Here you might need these when you catch up with those rustlers," he said unbuckling his favorite nickel-plated six-shooters in a fancy leatherwork holster that had been stolen in 1910 from a Famous Mexican General. He buckled the holster around his little daughter, as she mounted her trusty steed. "And don't forget your hat!" He placed the big cowboy hat on her head, which promptly drooped down over her eyes. "Hi Ho Silver, away!" she cried galloping off toward the window, raising one of the pistols in the air and firing off a round which embedded itself in the ceiling, knocking a big chunk of chalky plaster to the ground.

At the sound of the shot his secretary rushed in.

"On second thought, maybe you won't need those," said the President, taking the six-shooters away from his daughter. "Fix that, would you?" he said to his secretary who was relieved to see that the cause of the commotion was just the President's daughter firing a pistol at the ceiling, and that the only damage that had been done was that a chunk of plaster had fallen down. "And remind me to leave these down on the Ranch the next time," he said, giving his secretary the holster and six-shooters. With his Chief of Staff at his side, he strutted out of the room with that uber-confident strut that he had grown famous for.

Just as they were leaving a group of three Secret Service agents with their guns drawn rushed into the room. "Don't worry boys. It was just my daughter having a little fun," said the President to the Secret Service agents who looked up at the ceiling before they re-holstered their weapons. They started talking into their throat microphones while the President left the room with his Chief of Staff. One of them followed behind nervously, not quite sure that everything was in fact back to normal, since after all, a firearm had actually been discharged in the Oval

Office. But the President didn't seem to care. He was his usual nonchalant self.

They went straight to the basement Situation Room where the President began to receive a full briefing on what had happened that was causing the precarious national security situation.

"You remember several years ago when we were trying to save money and okay- ed the procurement of those strategic bombers with the single pilot seat, thinking that if we reduced the number of members of a flight crew needed, we wouldn't have so many salaries to provide for when they went on fail-safe duty?" the Air Force Chief of Staff asked the President. The President nodded. It had seemed like a good idea at the time. "Well it seems that one of our boys has taken one out for a joy ride," explained the Air Force Chief of Staff, fidgeting uncomfortably as he spoke.

"I see," said the Bad President, drumming his fingers on the table. "A nukular joy ride. That doesn't sound too good. *Hmmm...*" He paused for a moment thinking about the ramifications of what he had learned. "Well, at least it can't do my popularity ratings any harm, eh Wendell?" he said, elbowing his Chief of Staff, who was sitting next to him, in the ribs. His Chief of Staff winced at first and then cracked a funny little exasperated smile. No it wouldn't. They couldn't go any lower. They were already lower than any other President's in History. The only thing keeping the President's approval rating above absolute zero was statistical noise, and those people on the lunatic fringe of the population who always approved of the President no matter what he did, and perhaps, according to one rumor, those pollsters in charge of calculating the results who, the rumor had it, maybe fudged them a bit in order to make it look like things weren't quite so bad as they really were.

The phone rang. The National Security Advisor picked it up. "Yes.. yes, I see," he said speaking into it. He cupped his hand over the mouthpiece and turned to look at the President. "Mr. President, a NORAD flight controller has finally made radio contact with that errant bomber and its rogue pilot, a certain Colonel Joseph Shaker. It seems by stealing the plane he is trying to send a message protesting your plan to cancel the military's "Don't Ask, Don't Tell" policy."

The Chief of Staff piped in. "He appears to be one of those gay rights activists, Jack."

He knew it! There was an 'ist' behind this problem! Not only did this pilot commit unnatural, unspeakable, and ungodly acts, but he wanted to make it easier for others to do the same thing. Here was where the floodgates of anarchy might break wide open if they weren't careful. They had to nip this one in the bud.

"Patch me through to that pilot," said the President. The National Security Advisor spoke a few words into the phone and then handed it over to the President.

He hesitated for a moment and then spoke into the phone. "Son, don't do anything foolish up there. Your country needs you. Honestly we do. We need you back on the team to help fight those, those..." The Bad President hesitated for a minute to try and remember which one of the enemies on the list were up at the top of the list right that second. There were the Fasc*ists*, and the Commun*ists*, the terrror*ists*, the Islam*ists*, the violent extrem*ists*, and a whole passle of others. Name a problem and you would find an *ist* or an *iste* involved in it. He covered the microphone with his hand. "Who are we concerned with now?" he asked his Chief of Staff. "The violent *extremists*, Jack" said the Chief of Staff. "Oh, that's right," said the President with his hand still over the microphone. He took his hand off the microphone. "...the violent *extremists*, who wouldn't care if your mom ate dog shit every day for the rest of her life. Your mom, my mom, and everybody's mom. They're evil son, and we need you to help us get them, those no good, horse thievin' cattle rustlers."

"I understand you have a problem with our plans to get rid of Don't Ask, Don't Tell."

The pilots voice, sounding faraway, came through on the speaker.

"Yes Mr. President. I think its unfair. After all...." And then he went into a whole litany of reasons why he thought the policy was fair and good and why it would be a bad idea to change it. The Bad President listened with a tight smile on his lips, nodding and seeming to agree from time to time. Then he responded. "Well, bully for you, son! You've changed my mind! I won't rescind that policy after all!"

This was followed by a moment of shocked silence around the room, and on the phone. "You promise, Mr. President?" asked the gay bomber pilot who had stolen the bomber with the nuclear weapons aboard.

"Sure, kid. I promise," he said.

But of course the Bad President had no intention of keeping that promise. As soon as the gay rights activist landed he was going to be met by a contingent of heavily armed MP's, thrown in the brig, and face a serious court martial where no lawyer would ever do him any good. He would never have sex again, normal or otherwise, for the rest of his life. And then the silly ridiculous policy of "Don't Ask, Don't Tell" would be thrown onto the dung heap of history forever.

He marveled at his sheer audacity as President. He could lie his ass off, and no matter how often he did so, because he was President, people always believed him. What a great job! It was such a great job that, privately, he was thinking of ways he might be able to extend it beyond the end of his second term, perhaps by starting some kind of war and declaring martial law, but he hadn't told anyone about that yet.

"Now bring that bomber home where it belongs, son," he said.

"I will Mr. President. I will. And thank you!"

The president clicked off the phone. "What's wrong with that boy, anyway?" he asked.

His Chief of Staff shook his head. "I don't know. We're reaping the whirlwind, Mr. President. Reaping the whirlwind."

As they left the Situation Room and walked upstairs to the Oval Office, they passed a nude Renoir that had been given to the White House by the new French President, a gift from the French nation to the people of the United States. But there was a problem with the priceless painting which had once hung in the Louvre where millions of people had flocked to see it. It depicted a nude bather, combing her hair. The President, a devout, born-again Christian, did not like works of art with nudity in them. In fact, he hated them. He felt that having them in the hallways of government was an insult to the dignity and decorum that was expected of the institutions of government. And so while he had hung the nude bather on the wall so as not to insult the

French President or the people of the nation of France, he had ordered that a blanket be hung over it after the French President went back to France so that no one could see the nude bather's breasts or her lovely naked thighs. In the same spirit of sanctimony, all the other works of art on federal premises that had even a smidgen of nudity in them were similarly covered over with blankets, even the beautiful nude statute of the Goddess of Justice in the Justice Department Building. It was quite an odd thing to pass through the hallways of the federal buildings in Washington after the Inauguration and see so many paintings and statues covered over with blankets. But people had eventually grown used to it. One could not after all question the order of a President, even if he was a Bad President.

One might have had an inkling of how this man would behave toward nude art once he became President from his previous behavior. Before he had become President, and after he sold his major league baseball team for an obscene amount of money, the Bad President had been the titular President of a major University and had presided over the modernization of its campus, a project that he had loved because it had allowed him to rub shoulders with the rich alumni at cocktail parties during the development drive and not do too much actual work. During the construction activities attendant to the modernization process, a decision had to be made about the two green patina-ed, life-sized statues of naked women that were near the library. As they replaced all the lovely greenswards and gardens on campus with new asphalt parking lots and glass and steel buildings and concrete sidewalks, which cost tens of millions of dollars and put the University deeply into debt for the first time in its history (all at the urging of the ne'er-do-well President of course!), the project managers simply could not seem to find the right place to re-locate the statues which evoked the classical Greek statues of antiquity, and the high state of learning that had been present during that time, and which did not cost anybody anything because they had been donated eons ago.

Some people wanted to put them in storage, at least temporarily. But they were held in such great esteem by so many of the faculty who could not bear to see them go, that a decision that might have been made by the Campus Modernization Project Director had been kicked upstairs to the president's office.

"Scrap 'em," said the president, after he had heard his aide explain the delicate problem to him in detail.

"What? We can't do that! Those statues were a gift to the University by the illustrious Earl Peabody, Class of 1872! They have been on our campus for generations," said his aide somewhat indignantly, despite the fact that he knew he was addressing someone higher up.

"You heard me. I said scrap them. I'm President of this pop stand and I order you to contact the salvage yard immediately and sell them for whatever they will bring," the President said. The President had read earlier that day that scrap metals prices were up, and he thought he was being very wise in not just giving the sculptures away. Why the $2,000 or $3,000 they would get from the sale of the bronze would help to pay down the debt on the new buildings they were constructing. It wouldn't be much but it would be something, and he could point that out to anyone who might criticize his decision.

This had been just one of several instances where the Bad President's feelings towards nudity in art had expressed themselves before he became President of the United States, a country which at one time had been the most powerful nation on earth but which, under his leadership, rapidly went downhill. How far downhill? Lower than an inchworm's belly is a phrase that comes to mind.

Before he became President, the cold war had fizzled out, the arms race had ended, and all the world's strategic missiles had been pointed into the sea so that if one went off by accident, as such things might occasionally do, it would fall harmlessly into the water and not hurt anybody. The Nation's debt had been erased and there was a $6 trillion budget surplus. Everyone had a good job, money in their pocket, and around the world everybody loved America and wanted to come to visit.

But all that changed after the Bad President took over at the helm. The Bad President squandered the nation's treasure and prestige more than all the other terribly bad presidents before him. And after he became President, people became much less happy living in America. They thought about ways they could leave and live in other countries where he wasn't President. And people overseas decided they didn't want to come here. When Americans met Europeans overseas, perhaps at spas or at tables in cafes, the wise, world-weary Europeans would shake their heads slowly and say, "So sad what happened to America."

Why? Well, here's a 'for instance' for you. Under the Bad President, traveling in America became a lot less pleasant. Americans used to delight in their ability to travel freely around their own country without restriction. Whereas before you could get onto an airplane to see your girlfriend or cousin off and spend a few moments chatting with them before the big bird catapulted off into the wild blue yonder, now they wouldn't let your non-traveling friends even near the plane. So that if you wanted to spend a few extra moments with your loved ones they, too, had to buy an airplane ticket to Kalamazoo, even if they weren't going there, just so you could pass through the three different checkpoints to get to the waiting area near the plane's gate together where you would wait for the plane, which of course they weren't going to do because it would cost them too much money and because they'd be crazy to want to subject themselves to the numerous personal indignities involved just to say goodbye. And whereas before you could get onto a train and plop down into a seat without any hassles, and be left alone while you enjoyed your sandwich and a magazine on the 5 hour train ride to see Aunt Jane, without anybody questioning who you were or what you were..... because after all, wasn't that your own frigging business?.... now you were hassled every step of the way, from before you boarded, to after you got off the train in Peoria. Brutal men with automatic weapons, body armor, and black attack clothing strode back and forth like arrogant lunatics in the cars on the train. If they didn't like the way you looked, and they didn't like the way a lot of people looked because that was the kind of people they were, they could open up your bags and paw through them, shake their heads disapprovingly at your choice of underwear, thrown in there as an afterthought, perhaps, and/or confiscate anything that they didn't like or that was considered contraband at the moment, under whatever lunatic theory of the day was in effect. Although they rarely pointed their machine guns at people's heads, the threat that they might do so was clearly implied, and the sight of all that firepower and machinery of death filled even the most innocent traveler, perhaps somebody's 89 year old grandmother who had never done anything wrong in her life, with dread and unease. Indignity after indignity was suffered by Americans at the hands of their own government and Americans began to hate it, which was just what the Bad President and his henchmen wanted, even though they would never admit it, because hate and fear was what they thrived on, even though they tried to convince people that what they were doing was for their own safety and in their own best interests.

Like parrots, whenever anyone attempted to complain about all this un-American activity which was making the country a less fun and less secure place to live in, the Bad President and his henchmen would squawk: "Security!"... "Security!"... "Security!".."Security!... And they would say it like they had lumps of coal in their mouths with their low-down-frequency voices like they had learned to do, with an artificial *gravitas* that they hoped people would view as genuine, in that same slow-talking way that sounded like it came from straight out of the American heartland but really didn't. Like the broomsticks in the fairy tale of the Sorcerer's Apprentice, the fears engendered by the Bad President and nourished by his government started multiplying out of control. It seemed that just like the Sorcerer's Apprentice, the Bad President had mistakenly invoked a spell from a stolen book of incantations that he really didn't understand when he started to use the politics of fear to control the nation. It was, of course, the same book of incantations that had been used by that clever house painter from Austria who had led Germany down such a disastrous path in the 1930's. And if you went to Arlington Cemetery you could see a lot of graves of people who had fought the mind-controlled masses that had followed that madman. But now there were other masses of mind-controlled men and women who were following a different pied piper, but one who was blowing the same tune. The irony of this situation was lost on most people, but not on everyone. Lots of good people could see what was going on and didn't like it at all.

I should note that because of all the hassles, people traveled less. And because they traveled less, the ideas that they used to interchange with each other, the grand game of social intercourse, suffered mightily. Innovations in one part of the country were slower to take hold in other parts of the country. The country entered a deep malaise and things just seemed to get worse and worse with no end in sight. That is before the nude yard man came along, who of course changed everything. As we shall soon see, he began to accomplish this change using a very simple mode of travel that wasn't subject to any serious kind of oversight at all: all you had to do was stick out your thumb, and you could get *anywhere*.

7

The Oracle Dies and Charles Morgan Hitchhikes Out to Leigh Oilerman's

Although it sometimes seemed like she would live forever, one day the Oracle died, quite unexpectedly and quite suddenly. A small piece of tissue, a neuronal cell wall to be exact, in her temporal lobe that had been hit by an abnormally high energy cosmic ray particle when she was 7 years old, had gradually developed over the years into a lesion that produced sporadic epileptic fits. Each fit got bigger and bigger as the lesion and surrounding scar tissue grew. It was just a little tear at first and did not create any noticeable physiological effect for years and years when she was younger, but as she got into her middle years it became increasingly serious and life threatening as her body chemistry changed. She did not tell anybody about these violent neurological seizures that happened to her because she didn't want anybody to worry. Also, they scared her. She did not want to think about them. She knew that one day she would have a seizure and die. She knew it with the same inner certainty that everyone knows any deep inner truth. The doctors told her so, and she knew it, too. And so she did not want to think about it. She preferred to focus her attention on the things that made her happy in life.

The thing that made her the most happy in life was Uncle Winkle who lavished all sorts of attention on her. When the Oracle died, Uncle Winkle was cast into a deeply morose state. Nothing could bring him back from the black hole that had been created in his life with the death of his best friend and lover. "Go, I can teach you no more," he said to the nude yardman, who one day went over for his usual mathematics lesson. "I can teach no one anymore. For I am finished. *Kaput!* I am a body without a soul." And so the nude yardman, bowed his head very low, feeling terribly sorry for his Uncle Winkle, who was grief-stricken and in tears. And he put his hand on his shoulder for a little while. But he knew there was nothing he could do for him. And so he left.

Charles Morgan had now lost everyone in is family who was in a position to provide material and spiritual sustenance for him. His father to jail, his mother to who knows where, his grandmother to a nursing home (she had gone into one two months before), and his Uncle Winkle to melancholia and depression. What was he to do?

He decided to go out and visit "Uncle" Leigh Oilerman once again, and spend some time with him. Uncle Leigh was a very sensible fellow. He would know what to do. He was a good friend of the family and would never steer him wrong. So he went to the nursing home and told his grandmother that he was going out to see Uncle Leigh for awhile. His grandmother thought for a moment and then said, "Oh, well say hi to him for me." She did not actually know Leigh Oilerman but she was one of those people who thought it was always a good idea to say 'hi' to people anyway since she was a very kindly person. So Charles Morgan hitchhiked out to see "Uncle" Leigh who was a little bit surprised to see him, but not overly so.

During the second time he spent with Uncle Leigh, Charles Morgan did not do any gardening in the nude. He just didn't feel like doing it around Uncle Leigh. It didn't seem right. Uncle Leigh was a sort of prudish fellow, and he didn't want to make him feel uncomfortable. How could he tell him about The Dream? How could he tell him that the only way he could counter the demonic supernatural forces that were gunning for him in his mind all the time was to take off all his clothes and garden in the nude again? He wouldn't understand.

****

Uncle Leigh's Advice on Planting Ginseng

First off, be very careful when handling the rootlets. Never handle the rootlets roughly or without care. They will KNOW when they are being handled roughly. Inspect the ginseng when you first receive it. Notice how the rootlets look like little 'beings'. The resemblance to humans is uncanny. Ginseng is called the "manroot" because of its homologous human quality.

It is also called the "mainroot" because of its central place in her-bology. Thinking of each little rootlet as a 'being' is useful when you are planting ginseng. The trick is to lay it into the ground so that it is anatomically perfect and 'comfortable' during its 10 year stay underground.

Ginseng needs to be planted on a hillside where lots of mature hardwood trees are. There is some sort of interaction which goes on in the forest between the ginseng and the trees. Sounds like bs, I know. But it's true. Ginseng grown under artificial shade is not as powerful as that grown in the shade of the forests.

Ginseng likes the shade. The optimum growing temperature is 55 degrees Fahrenheit, which strangely is also the temperature at which the human brain works best.

Use the claw of a claw hammer or a claw-shaped digging device to clear out a fist-sized hole for the ginseng rootlet to grow in. Get rid of all the rocks and other obstacles to growth like other roots. The forest floor humus should be slightly moist. Two inches is a good depth. A little more or a little less is okay. Remember to give the little rootlet plenty of room to grow in. The more room it has, the bigger it will grow. And plant it on a gentle slope so that it is properly drained.

✳✳

So it was sort of awkward for Charles Morgan to spend time with "Uncle" Leigh at this time. Awkward for both of them. Uncle Leigh didn't know exactly what Charles Morgan expected from him. And neither did Charles Morgan know exactly why he was there. And it was even more awkward because he could not tell him about The Dream. But one night as he was laying awake he heard the wind chimes that were hung from a low-lying branch of the pine tree on the edge of the forest by Leigh's house begin an actual symphony that seemed like it was meant for him. It was as if a benevolent spirit had taken possession of the chimes to play him a song to let him know that everything was going to be alright. And Charles Morgan, as he lay there astounded that such things could happen, that actual, beautiful, human-sounding music could be produced where only statistical noise should have been present, suddenly had a revelation. "Oh, so that's why I am here," he said to himself. "To learn that benevolent supernatural forces do exist in life, and that they actually do try to communicate with you in their own special way! Wow, isn't that interesting!" The next day, filled with the energy from his realization, he told Uncle Leigh that he decided he was going to leave and hitch-hike around the country for awhile to work at odd landscaping jobs and see the sights.

8

Travels Far and Wide

Like Forest Gump who one day decided to run, it was on that day that Charles Morgan decided to hitchhike. If he wanted to see Mount Rushmore and see the solemn, granite faces of those august former Presidents with their stern visages, he would just head out to Rapid City, North Dakota and see them. If he wanted to see Yosemite National Park, he would go there. If he wanted to spend some time on the cool beaches of North Carolina, you guessed it. He would point his compass in that direction and set sail, with no one to tell him otherwise. He had liked hitch-hiking out to Uncle Leigh's. It was the first big hitchhike he had tried and he liked it, and wanted to try more of it. It gave him a sense of freedom. He had finished high school and was unencumbered with any responsibilities which restricted him to one place. He had no home, no 9-5 job, no pets, no steady girl-friend. And heading out on his own would rid his psyche of the terrible feeling of awkwardness that he had developed around

Uncle Leigh's. Oh what a crazy, foolish, glorious, courageous decision he made! Oh what a unique path he chose, emboldened by the Good Spirit of the Wind Chimes! That was the sign that allowed him to form a clean break with an otherwise ordinary past. And it was because Charles Morgan kept an eye on his soul that he was able to see to see it for what it was: a path to true enlightenment. Others, too distracted by events in the material world might have missed that little lacunae of spiritual insight. But not Charles Morgan! No siree! He grabbed it like it was the best opportunity of his life. And it was! You need to be paying attention when God speaks to you!

This period in his life has been compared with the 'missing years' of Jesus's life, except that we know so little of what Jesus did during this period that to draw too strong a parallel might prove pointless. Certainly we know that Jesus was not hitch-hiking. Or was he? Certainly it is possible that he did "hitch" rides on camel caravans here and there around Judea, Chaldea, and Hindustan at that time. So we will just leave it at that, except perhaps to speculate that what Jesus was learning in those remote, snowy monasteries of Tibet,[4] during at least a part of those missing years, Charles Morgan was learning on the highways and byways of America: a kind of deep spiritual insight that transcended the age, and defied all attempts at conventional, fact-based understanding.

For you see, it was during this period of hitchhiking that Charles Morgan *really* got to know people. And they got to know him. And as opposed to Ishmael, about whom it was said in the Bible, *"His hand will be against every man, and every man's hand against him"*, for Charles Morgan, during this period of hitchhiking and then beyond, the opposite was true: *"His hand was with every man, and every man's hand with him."* (And of course every woman's, too!)

That such a saying might be reserved for a true Messiah is indeed possible. But it started off in a much more mundane fashion. Because when you are hitchhiking you see, you cannot afford to offend anybody. You are entirely at their mercy and you don't want to say or do anything to offend them for fear they will pull over to the side of the road and ask you to get out of the car in a fit of pique and leave you stranded. So you don't. And neither can the person giving you a ride afford to say or do anything to offend you because they don't know whether you are really an ax murderer or a serial killer or a deeply disturbed psychotic who is merely putting up a good show of normality to get a ride, and they don't want you to suddenly pull a gun out of your pocket in a similar fit of pique and then force you over in some remote place, take your money and your car, and then roar off to who knows where leaving you stranded by the side of the road without your cell phone, your wallet, or your dignity. So they don't. There are thus automatic confines to the transaction which help the parties start off on the right foot with each other without any need for messianic virtue to be involved.

Each party starts off being extremely deferential to the other, and especially nice, in an exaggerated sort of way that is not present in normal business transactions. Certainly it might be true that the hitchhiker tries to be nice a little harder than the driver, because it is realized that he is after all receiving a tangible benefit, i.e., transportation down the road, without paying for it. So he tries to be a little nicer than he is ordinarily in life by offering his best version of pleasant conversation and company to the often-times-as-not solitary driver, trying his darndest to bestow a little warmth and human companionship where before there was none in the previously cold, empty seat that he is now sitting in. That is the coin of the realm with which he attempts to pay for the ride. But the driver, not being a pompous ass by definition (for if he were, would he have pulled over to pick up the poor hitchhiker in the first place?) tries to be a little nicer than he normally is also, because he realizes that the hitchhiker is probably down on his luck, otherwise why would he be hitch-hiking, and that accepting charity from a perfect stranger is always somewhat awkward; and that it might be him who was down on his luck and needed the ride, after all!

In order to counter the awkwardness deriving from his charity, the driver is eager not to be a perfect stranger to the hitchhiker, and so he tries, perhaps overly hard, to be companionable and friendly, and to reveal parts of his life to the hitchhiker that he might not reveal them to anyone else, perhaps even his spouse. Their meeting is a compressed moment of intimacy. Deep memories are stirred by this random encounter. Philosophical truths universally recognized are relied upon for all pronouncements. And risks are taken in conversation and behavior that would not ordinarily be taken to quickly establish genuine friendship. They are taken quickly, because there is not much time to determine whether or not the hitchhiker you have picked up, or the seemingly nice driver who has picked you up, is not really a depraved, vicious con-man-serial-killer simply masquerading as an ordinary person, simply waiting for the right time to rob you or rape you or kill you in some horrible grotesque fashion involving lots of blood and suffering....the sooner you find that out the better!... and genuine, because if that other person *is* such a depraved individual, you hope that by being so nice you will be one of the lucky ones he spares during his depraved crime spree.

Now it should be said that the incidence of such depraved killers in our society is extremely low, much less so than the newspapers would have us believe. But there is always the possibility....after all, there are all those stories and stereotypes in the movies... that try your darndest, you cannot get them out of your mind for the first several minutes of the hitchhiking encounter...so that you rely, by a sort of default, and by a calculated prudence, and by longstanding hitchhiking tradition, on good karma to carry you through such a moment of personal vulnerability, like when you jump out of an airplane with a parachute and ask god for a little forbearance for your sins.

As they struggle to establish each other's *bona fides* in as short a time as possible, with whatever crude or refined social skills they might possess, the air between the hitchhiker and driver is filled with rich, colorful conversation. Few relationships struck up so suddenly and spontaneously can claim to be so verbal. As mentioned before, such conversation is necessary for both parties because it has survival value. It is necessary to appraise and to dispel their animal fear of that other person, sitting so close by, who, by virtue of their physical proximity to you and the unique circumstances of the encounter (there are, for instance, no other people in the world, generally, who know that they have come together) could do so much harm so quickly.

Just like the farmer learns the hard way not to sow his seeds in the Spring before the last threat of frost is passed, and the banker learns not to extend credit to people of questionable character, the hitchhiker learns not to bring up topics that might cause a rift in the initial peace and mutual trust which exists a priori between hitchhiker and driver. The driver senses the same thing. And so the conversation between them is usually extremely agreeable. There are of course moments of silence during which each party sits side by side without saying much of anything, while they digest, perhaps, what they have learned about the other person, or enjoy the scenery. But as often as not such moments come about naturally without any awkwardness at all.

Hitchhikers get to know people as they really are in their travels around the country. It is not the sort of relationship that makes for any sort of phoniness, ostentation, or deceit. As a rule, there is the potential for such initially casual encounters to grow into personal relationships of the highest caliber, and many lifelong friendships have developed between hitchhikers and their rides. Certainly until their dying day, most people can remember each and every person they met when hitchhiking, so sharpened are their senses by the circumstances of the meet.

And it is an amazing, and truly remarkable commentary on the human condition, that such random encounters between individuals who might be as different as the sun and the moon, could take root and blossom into such intimate relationships so quickly and last so long. Perhaps you've heard of the lifelong friendship that developed between musicians Townes Van Zandt and Joe Ely that began when Ely picked up Van Zandt hitchhiking in Texas with 30 vinyl LP's of his newest record in a dusty backpack by his feet? That's certainly one example.

These things he would learn eventually, but initially, the desire to head out on the road had only to do with the fact that deep down, Charles Morgan was filled with a determination to make it on his own, without any financial help from anybody. Houdini had left home at the age of 12. Edison at the age of 14. Louis Lamour at 15. Certainly he could make it on his own at 18 if those other fellows had managed at far younger ages. Mohamed had even lost his father when he was a baby, for heaven's sake and it hadn't affected his rise to greatness. So he set out with the $200 he had in his backpack from Uncle Leigh's, and took odd jobs in all the small little towns he came into, or from the people who gave him rides, and stayed with them, too, if they invited him to, or in tents in campgrounds.

As he traveled around he taught many people how to do yardwork in the nude. And they in turn taught many others.

During this phase of his life Charles Morgan considered it his true vocation to bring nude yard working to the masses, the plain and fancy people, the people of America. If he was working as a dishwasher in a diner in Wichita, he would make friends with the people in the town, the receptive ones, anyway, and teach them nude yard working. If he got a job in a Seattle suburb mowing lawns or tending gardens, he would make friends with the people he met in the library or at the post office, and make a date to teach them all the tricks he knew about the subject, what kneepads to use, what hand-spades lasted the longest, what the best suntan oil was for outdoor work, etc., all the while planting radishes, pumpkins, or tomatoes. If, while reading *USA Today* over his morning coffee, he read about a person in another part of the country who had experienced a tragedy in their lives, like their son had been killed in a war, or their lover had leapt from a cliff, or their spouse had been killed in a plane crash, or their house had burned down in a fire, Charles Morgan would say to himself, "Hmmph! Now that person knows enough to stop taking life for granted! But what they don't know about is nude yard working!" And he would quietly wind up his affairs in the town he was in and set out, hitch-hiking, to visit that person or family and clue them in to the benefits of nude yard work, for who else was going to do it?

Charles Morgan had such a way with people that almost no one refused his offers of help. Generally they would immediately admire his amazing serenity and ask him about it. How is it that you remain so calm in these troubled times, this vast sea of socio-economic turbulence that America has never experienced before, they would ask. They inevitably got around to this question and when they did..aha! ..that was like a door opening to their souls through which Charles Morgan could proceed and spread his message. "I do yard work in the nude," he would say, shrugging his shoulders, intimating that perhaps there was an explanation, a secret recipe for his success, that most others did not know about, but also one that was as simple and obvious as falling off a log. And one that everyone could do if they wanted to. He said it in the same way that he might have said "I pray everyday underneath the old oak tree" or "I do a good deed every day" or "I use Dr. Bonner's soap". That was all it took. And they invariably started thinking "Hey, if he can do yard work in the nude and it has such a positive impact on him, why can't I?" That was all it took for them to begin their own experiments with naked yard work. Sometimes they did it the same day that they had their conversation with Charles Morgan. And sometimes they waited till the weekend. But try it they did.

The "germination ratio" was near 80% for gardeners, and 50% for others who hadn't tried gardening before. And of course once they tried it, they were hooked on it for it really was an enjoyable, cost-free thing to do, which added years to your life, made you healthier, and increased your sex drive appreciably. Plus there were all those delicious vegetables to eat that came as a bonus! Tomatoes, potatoes, asparagus, beets, and squash! There was no real downside to doing yard work in the nude, except being uncomfortable when it was cold outside and this could be guarded against by that most simple expedient of all: simply not doing it when it was too cold outside, or coming inside afterwards and having a nice hot toddy!

People in America were simply ready for nude yard working when Charles Morgan came along. They were fed up with politics, civic association/community involvement seemed pointless, and the 565 channels of television that they could get on their cable and streaming providers were a wasteland, filled with assassin movies, vampire episodes, and depressing world and national news that wasn't much fun to watch. Furthermore, they were tired of nameless, faceless corporations getting away with murder and ruling their lives. The fabled 'System' had forgotten about them; it seemed like it had run amok. They needed something new and productive in their lives that they could count on. Something they could feel good about. Something they could do on their own. And nude yard working seemed to fit the bill. It fit right into that empty space in their lives. It felt great! And that's why it caught on so well.

Many times Charles Morgan took jobs with local landscapers when he hitchhiked into a town. They had a voracious appetite for day laborers. Some of these guys were hardworking, fair and good to work for. And some weren't. So he learned to recognize the bad actors in the landscaping profession and to avoid them. The archetype of the pushy, dishonest landscape contractor existed, just like the archetype of the overly aggressive general contractor did, the ones who submitted low-ball estimates, milked a job for all it was worth, and then bullied their generally meek clients into paying inflated bills, padded with all sorts of inflated items.

He learned to recognize these predators by their expensive, late model pickup trucks with the slick advertising signs (which were generally never fully paid for), and the yellow-sheened, bug-like sunglasses which they wore. Those were the guys to be avoided. They would talk a great game and get you to work for them for what they said would be fabulous wages, and then when it came time to pay you they would only give you half of what you were owed, using excuses like you didn't do the job correctly, or they were still owed money from a previous job and didn't have the money to pay you that week, and if you didn't like it you were free to find another job, etc. etc. etc.

But he never had any trouble with the people who wanted to learn nude yard working from him. And all in all he managed to keep his head well above water, financially, during this time because he had so few fixed expenses.

After a year of hitchhiking around the country, he had saved up what amounted to a decent pile of money doing odd jobs, mostly in the landscaping field, $3,407. Since the average person had only $800 in the bank, and was much older than he was, Charles Morgan, who was only 19, felt very proud of himself.

He realized this when he was traveling with his friend Saunders about 50 miles outside of Denver on Interstate 80. They were traveling eastbound in a car that as their hitchhiking luck would have it, belonged to a recent releasee from the Denver mental hospital, Crazy Mickey they called him. Charles Morgan had just counted his money in his backpack, sitting in the back of Mickey's car.

"Do you realize, you two, that I have $3,407 sitting in this backpack and I would like to spend some of it to celebrate my good fortune with you? Will you accept my invitation to have a nice big meal at the next restaurant we come to?"

Saunders yawned. "OK, Charles," he said. Saunders was the same age as the Nude Yardman, and dressed pretty much like him. They had met at a party in Boulder at the Naropa Institute.

Saunders had made his first million trading foreign currencies on an on-line software program he had inadvertently found on his older brother's computer. He had clicked on an interesting looking icon on the computer's desktop and up popped a fully live version of a foreign exchange trading platform, loaded with $10,000 in freshly deposited cash, and approved for 400:1 leverage. His brother had never figured anybody else would use his computer since it was in his bedroom. He had set the OS to remember the username and password on that account so he could log in more easily, which is how Saunders came upon it.

Saunders was an *idiot savante*. Numbers just meant more to him than they did to the average person, even the average person who was good at math. Numbers and combinations of numbers. So when he saw all those currency quotations flashing on the screen, he went wild with joy. In about 5 minutes he could discern trading patterns which affected the price movements of the currency pairs that not even the best supercomputers in the world could detect. He couldn't help himself. In about 4 hours of trading he had racked up profits of $1,373,285. That was when his older brother came into his bedroom and discovered Saunders on his computer, who was logged into his trading account without permission.

Saunders' brother went ballistic. He started hitting Saunders to get him out of the chair, and Saunders, not understanding this attack at all, fell off the chair, and then ran out of the room with his brother chasing him, yelling and screaming. When his brother came back and saw what Saunders had done for his account value, he felt suddenly nauseous. What a complete asshole he had been! Saunders, deeply hurt, disappeared for 3 weeks hitchhiking, never sleeping a wink during the whole time. When he did return his brother tried to get Saunders to trade his account for him again, this time with permission and with the intent of making money for both of them. In fact, he begged him. But Saunders refused to do so. Deep down inside his soul where things hurt the most he had been psychologically traumatized. Whenever someone mentioned on-line trading of foreign currency, and implored him to make the same kind of money he had made for his brother in those four hours of numinous numerological ecstasy, he cringed markedly, remembering the beating he had taken from doing so. In Saunders' brain, which was wired a little differently than the rest of ours (he was not a 'neurotypical' at all), he associated the activity with the event of the beating more strongly than the thrill and satisfaction of making all that money. The money came from the numbers, and the numbers were just numbers. By reading their patterns, he was just doing what came naturally to him, so the fact of making the money had not imprinted too strongly on his brain. But the beating! Ay-yay-yay! That he remembered! And so Saunders refused to ever trade foreign currencies again for anybody, no matter how sweetly they enticed him. (Thank god for the rest of the world's foreign currency traders, because if Saunders had ever decided to trade again, they would all have been bankrupted!) Eventually, after a few days at home, seeing nothing on the home front that interested him, Saunders lit out hitching again in an avid fashion, liking the romance of the road, which is how he had connected with Charles Morgan in Boulder.

"Mickey? How about you? Will you accept my invitation to join me in celebration of my first year on my own?" Charles Morgan asked.

Mickey was watching a lime green convertible pass by on the other side of the road. "Yeah, sure, of course." He was busy driving, so he didn't get too excited about it, one way or the other.

After driving a little further down the Interstate, they came to a rest stop with a decent-looking restaurant in it. They stopped and got out of the car. As they were going into the restaurant to eat, Charles Morgan noticed a forlorn-looking girl sitting in a booth all by herself with a little cupcake in front of her, with a single, lit birthday candle sticking up in it. She looked like she had just been crying. Their eyes met.

"There, there, young lass. Do not fret! What's the matter?" Charles Morgan asked.

The girl looked up at Charles Morgan and sniffled. "It's my birthday and I have no one to celebrate it with and I'm all alone in this wretched, roadside restaurant. And I have no money for lunch."

She sounded so desperate and pathetic that all of a sudden her plight kindled Charles Morgan's charitable instincts. He reached into his backpack and handed her a $20 bill.

"Here. I hope this helps," Charles Morgan said, wondering whether he should do more to help the young girl.

Saunders came up from behind him and grabbed his elbow. "This way, partner. I found us a table." He steered the Nude Yardman over to a booth where Mickey was already sitting, looking at the menu. They both sidled into their seats.

"What gives, Saunders?" Charles Morgan asked. "I was having a conversation with that gal, and you butted in."

"Just trying to do you a favor," Saunders replied.

"What do you mean?"

"That girl over there? It wasn't her birthday."

"Huh? How do you know?"

"Or you could say it was her "birthday", and that she has 365 "birthdays" in a row every year. It's the old cupcake and birthday candle trick. That girl is a professional grifter. Tomorrow she'll be sitting over there in that same booth, with that same cupcake and candle and forlorn look on her face, telling the next guy who comes in who'll listen to her that its her birthday, that she's all alone, and that she's broke. She makes quite a good living that way. She'll take your money and spend it on cigarettes or her cellphone bill, or bailing an abusive boyfriend out of jail for the umpteenth time."

"Wow, what a scam! How did you know?"

"A trucker told me about that. As you know, from time to time they can be great founts of knowledge when it concerns the lore of the road." Saunders considered his fingertips, and decided his nails were pretty clean and not long enough to clip. "Oh yes, they can be mighty rough on you out here.... Imagine that! Pretending its your birthday and duping someone into giving you money like that!" He shook his head contemplating The Dark Side of Human Nature, thankful that so many truck drivers of the world were his friends, and that they freely shared their wisdom with him when he was hitchhiking.

"A cheeseburger special," Mickey said to the waitress who had come over to take their order.

Charles Morgan and Saunders added their orders to the list and the waitress went into the kitchen singing a song that only she could clearly hear or understand.

"What happens if you come in here another day, and you find her doing it again when you think it's not her birthday and you confront her about it?" Charles Morgan asked.

"She'll tell you to scram, and mind your own business. In a different tone of voice, of course," Saunders said.

For an *idiot savante*, Saunders was remarkably street smart. It paid to be a good friend of truck drivers the way he was. They didn't know it, but absolutely everything they told him he added to his eidetic memory. Saunders was a walking encyclopedia of trucker lore, just like he remembered the names of all of the people who had given him rides. If you've seen the movie *Rainman* and remember the part where Dustin Hoffman starts recalling all the airplane crashes that happened, you get the picture.

Their lunch came and they ate heartily. Afterward, as they were drinking their coffee, Saunders took out a pack of cards and shuffled them perfectly, the way they teach you in the best casinos in the world. "Anybody want to play cards?" Saunders asked.

"Saunders!" Charles Morgan said indignantly. "You remember every single card that's dealt! Asking people to play cards with you is like that girl over there telling people its her birthday!"

Saunders sighed. "Yeah, but the difference is I'm your buddy," said Saunders wistfully. He hadn't expected anybody to take him up on the offer. But he felt like he had to ask.

They got back in the car and headed East. After a while, Mickey spoke.

"You know, I'll bet I know what you really are," he said to Charles Morgan looking at him in the mirror. "You're a con artist. And you," he said shifting his gaze to look at Saunders in the mirror. "I'll bet I can tell what you are, too."

"What's that Mickey?"

"A hit man!"

Saunders snorted.

"I'm not a hit man, Mickey," Saunders said.

"And I'm not a con man!" said Charles Morgan.

"Then just what are you?" asked Mickey.

"I'm just an ordinary person, that's all," said Charles Morgan. "And so's Saunders." Saunders nodded his head.

Suddenly Mickey pulled the car over to the side of the road amid a screech of the brakes and a cloud of road dust. Then he opened his door and got out. "Come on out, you two. I want to show you something." The two hitchhikers got out of the car and accompanied Mickey to the rear of the car where he opened the trunk. He reached down into its cool darkness and pulled out a Size 42 Louisville Slugger baseball bat with his name, "Mickey Trudeau" engraved on it in perfect longhand script, burnt into the burnished ash stick with a machine-driven electric pen. It was a souvenir bat. "You see that," He pointed to his name. "That's my name." Then he raised the heavy souvenir bat up as if to swing at the two hitchhikers. "And as sure as my name's Mickey Trudeau, I'm going to beat you two senseless unless you tell me the truth.... Now, are you a con man...and are you a hitman...or aren't you?"

Charles Morgan and Saunders looked at each other wide-eyed. They didn't need any further convincing that the Denver mental hospital was currently full-up, and that the reason Mickey had been released was not because he had been cured, but because there were no open beds available.

Charles Morgan spoke. "You're right, Mickey. We may as well confess. I am a con man, and Saunders here, well, he is a hit man."

"Why didn't you just say so in the first place."

"I don't know Mickey, you don't just go around telling people those things, do you? It doesn't seem right. Does it? Now how did you guess the truth?"

"I'm never wrong about people. Never. Plus you had all that money in your bag. And ole' Saunders here, well he just reminds me of a hitman I once met. Something about his eyes. That shifty, far away look."

Saunders gulped. Then Mickey lowered the bat. "Well I guess we can get on down the road some more, now that you've told me the truth... I can't stand people riding around with me who don't tell me the truth." With that, he put the bat back in the trunk and slammed it shut.

Charles Morgan and his friend Saunders both sighed with relief and got back into the car glad that their mentally unstable friend was feeling better.

"You got any money for gas?" Mickey asked a short time later. He was looking at the gas gauge and the needle was moving rapidly to 'Empty'. He flicked it with his forefinger to make sure it wasn't stuck. After he flicked it it still read empty. Even he, in his mentally addled state, did not consider that a good thing.

"Not me," Saunders said. Saunders never carried any money. His brother had eventually set him up with half the winnings he had made on his foreign exchange account, and Saunders could have carried an ATM card along with him when he went hitchhiking but he preferred not to. He only carried American Express travelers checks. And it being the 21st Century, in America, not many people cashed them or even knew what they were. But that's the way he was. It was part of his sickness, you see, the nature of his being an *idiot savante*, that he did things in his own peculiar way, whether they made sense or not. He liked American Express, and he loved Karl Maldin. He wasn't going to travel with cash when he could travel with American Express traveler's checks! Cards could be hacked. But try hacking an American Express travelers check!

Sometimes Charles Morgan got mad at his friend for never having any money with him to pay their bills, even though he had plenty in the bank. But on this particular day Charles Morgan was feeling magnanimous. He gently admonished his friend, "You know if my friend Mary knew about the way you are, she'd tell me to have nothing to do with you!"

He handed Mickey two twenties out of the money in his pack. "Here you go Mickey. That ought to get us down the road a piece. Don't you have any money?"

"I think I do. In the bank. We ought to stop and see." So at a nearby exit Mickey got off and drove to the satellite branch of a bank that was near the highway. He parked the car and got out. Our two heros marched across the asphalt parking lot into the cool interior of the bank with him. There were potted plants (fake) in the lobby and a row of teller's windows over on the far side. Mickey went up to one of the windows and started talking to one of the tellers. Charles Morgan and Saunders tagged along, wondering where this was going. After all, the bank they had stopped at seemed pretty random. Was this indeed a branch of the bank where Mickey kept his money? Or was this some kind of joke? They didn't know but they had to give him the benefit of the doubt because Mickey did seem to have that kind of karma where he might be driving down a random stretch of highway and suddenly have one of his bank branches pop up out of nowhere. Furthermore, he was their driver. And except for the annoyance of burdening them with having to tell fake stories of hitman and conman exploits for the next couple of hours, he seemed like an ok guy, even if he did seem to be a couple sandwiches short of a picnic basket sometimes.

"I'd like to withdraw some of my money," said Mickey.

"Fine sir," the middle-aged female teller who had one lazy eye responded. Can I have your account number?"

"No. Sorry. I forgot it."

"Do you have any checks with you?" the teller with the lazy eye that looked like it was looking off to the side and yet at you at the same time said.

"No, I used them all."

"What's your name, sir? Perhaps I can find your account that way."

"Mickey,...Mickey Trudeau."

"I do find a "Mickey Trudeau" in our database, sir. However, I'll need to see some identification to make sure that you and he are the same person."

"Like a driver's license or credit cards or something?"

"I need two forms of government-issued picture ID sir."

"Well, gosh, when I got my driver's license they didn't put your picture on it. I got it 10 years ago and its good for five more years. You don't want me to have to spend $100 just to get another license when this one's still good, do you? And as far as something else goes, I don't have anything else."

"I'm sorry, sir. Without two forms of government-issued picture ID I'm afraid there's no way I can help you." She was losing her patience because the "Mickey Trudeau" she had looked up in her database only had $1.76 on deposit. And it wouldn't be long before his account was closed automatically anyway, and the money confiscated by the bank. That is unless he overdrafted, in which case fat overdraft fees would be accumulated against him in addition to the overdraft amount. She had seen it all before. She didn't know why the bank even did business with guys like him.

"Could you please move out of the line sir. There are other people I might have to help." It was a slow day at the bank and she was secretly reading a Danielle Steel novel behind the window, which she wanted to get back to.

Without meaning to, exactly, the middle aged teller with the lazy eye spoke in a rather snooty fashion, in a way that made Mickey, who had an over-developed sensibility about the way people treated him, kind of mad. Mickey looked behind him. There was nobody there. And the other tellers' windows were empty too.

"Humph!!' said Mickey. "I guess I need to teach this teller some manners. I guess I will have to read her the Riot Act, and introduce her to the good old Staff of Justice." He meant, of course, his souvenir Louisville Slugger. Which in a way was another form of ID since it had his name on it. "You two stay here," he said to Charles Morgan and Saunders.

Mickey turned on his heels, and went out to his car and reached into the cool darkness of his trunk where his one true treasure lay safely hidden, like some sort of secret dream of his disturbed, animal sub-conscious, and brought it out. Then he marched into the bank, where he had exactly $1.76 on deposit, or at least the Mickey Trudeau who was on their records did, to talk to the teller again.

"Listen Lady! I want *my* money!" he said brandishing his 'deadly weapon', swinging it up high above him like he was his namesake New York Yankees hero Mickey Mantle swinging for a game-winning home run in Fenway Park against the Red Sox on the last night of an imaginary World Series. "You see that name up there burned into the end of that bat? Mickey Trudeau! That's what it says! And that's who I am! Now do you believe me, or not?"

"Oh my god!" she said before she fainted. Two guards rushed over with their guns drawn and pointed them at Mickey who looked like he was attempting to rob the bank with a baseball bat. The two heroes, Charles Morgan and Saunders, sensing danger, jumped out of the way and landed under a writing desk on the floor, with their arms over their heads and squinching their eyes shut as tightly as they could to avoid getting splattered with parts of Mickey brain when the bullets started flying (as they were sure they would). Each one of them, unconsciously, starting curling into little balls like wooly bears do when you pick them off a leaf and hold them in your hand in order to minimize the target areas of their torsos.

Fortunately the guards could tell that Mickey wasn't a dangerous bank robber but merely a crazy nut with a baseball bat who had somehow wandered in off the street. One of them said, "Look bud, we don't want no trouble. Just put that baseball bat down, would ya?"

Their training told them that 5 out of 7 guys could be talked out of committing violence when confronted with point blank firepower in the form of weapons drawn and pointed at them. Mickey looked like he was one of those five. Mickey looked at them and then at the guns they had drawn which were pointed at him and realized all of a sudden that he had had one of his psychotic episodes and had been a bad boy. "Oh dear," said Mickey to himself aloud so that the guards could hear him. "I guess you fellows don't want to play ball," he said in the perpetual stream of consciousness that was his normal way of talking, and normal for most other schizophrenics as well.

"Guess I better put this bat down, eh?" he asked timidly, as he lowered the bat and dropped it on the floor.

"That's a good boy," said one of the guards. "Now would you mind sitting down next to it and putting these on, he threw a pair of handcuffs over to Mickey who sat down and put them on.

"You with anybody else?" the same guard asked.

"Yeah, those two,"said Mickey, pointing to Saunders and Charles Morgan who were starting to get up.

"No way! We don't know that guy! I mean we do know him, but not very well. He just picked us up hitchhiking, 50 miles back on the Interstate. We didn't know he was going to come in here and try and rob the bank!" Charles Morgan pleaded. Saunders' eyes started rolling up into his head and he began to tremble. It looked like he was going to have a seizure he was so nervous about what was happening. Being falsely accused of something is never easy and being falsely accused about being a bank robber in the middle of a bank robbery is even worse.

"Can you prove it?" the other guard asked.

Charles Morgan looked at Saunders and Saunders interrupted his seizure long enough to look back into Charles Morgan's eyes in alarm as if to say, 'How the heck are we ever going to prove that?'

Charles Morgan didn't answer. "Well, when the sheriff comes, you're going to have to explain it all to him," said the taller guard, keeping his gun pointed at them.

When the sheriff and his deputies came to secure the scene, they were taken down to the station with Mickey and put in a holding cell. A deputy rummaged through Charles Morgan's belongings and found the $3,407 (minus the amount he had spent on lunch and the money he had given the girl with the cupcake and birthday candle and the $40 he had given Mickey for gas) in cash he had in his knapsack, and held the wad of cash up for the sheriff to see. "Where the hell did you get this?" the sheriff who arrested them asked. "Say, are you boys serial bank robbers?" the sheriff asked, one of his eyebrows arching.

Charles Morgan yelled at Mickey who was in another cell. "You see what you did Mickey? Tell them Mickey! Tell them we weren't really with you when you tried to rob the bank, will you?" But Mickey was too despondent to talk. He wasn't talking to anybody. His neurological chemistry had swung into new, uncharted territory and no one knew how long it would be before he returned to normal.

Sensing no help from Mickey, Charles Morgan tried to shoulder the burden himself with the truth.

"I earned it, Sheriff," Charles Morgan said to the sheriff. "That's the fruit of one long year of hard work and savings. I earned it hitchhiking around the country doing yard work. I promise you I did."

"Yeah, sure kid. And my name's Donald Duck," said the sheriff who hated liars as much as he hated litterbugs, people who didn't vote, and people over 50 who went to Taylor Swift concerts. "Well, this here's going to be confiscated as evidence. You bet your bippy it is." He threw the knapsack in a tall steel safe that was standing against the wall. Then he shut the door and spun the dial on the combination lock. Charles Morgan's heart sank. His hard earned money, which represented the fruit of a full year of hitchhiking and doing odd yard work jobs with all the good people he had run into, had suddenly, and most unrighteously, disappeared right in front of his eyes.

After 2 days of bread and water (read: terrible jailhouse food), and the unbearable monotony of their holding cells, Mickey finally came around and admitted that Charles Morgan and Saunders were not his accomplices in the apparent bank robbery. And he held back on saying anything about what he thought their true professions to be, i.e., con man and hit man. But unfortunately the judge who they went before would not accept this testimony right off the bat (pardon the pun!) because Mickey appeared to be pretty nearly insane, and as is well known, insane persons do not always have a version of the facts that comports with reality. So he ordered a psychiatrist to examine Mickey, and to forward his findings to him. Then he would decide what to do with the lot of them.

Within a week, a letter arrived from the Denver mental hospital that said Mickey had been a patient there but had been released after an interview that had determined, among other things, that while Mickey appeared somewhat disturbed sometimes, his mental state did not in fact meet Colorado's legal standard of insanity, and that therefore he had been released (they didn't mention the lack of available beds). The psychiatrist, who had requested this letter, included it with its authoritative letterhead in his report to the judge. He also found that while Mickey appeared to suffer from periodic delusions, and severe childhood regression (hence the reliance made on the baseball bat), his was a harmless form of mental illness, if indeed you could even call it that. It could easily be kept under control with observation and the correct medication. The court corroborated this latter fact by reading a half dozen or so 'disturbing the peace' misdemeanors that Mickey had been guilty of over the years that were on his record, none of which involved any actual violence or injury to others. They were just minor, petty disturbances. This made him, in the judge's eyes somewhat more believable, and lent credence to his testimony. He didn't believe him 100%, however, because in his world, normal people did not walk into bank lobbies brandishing baseball bats demanding money and causing innocent tellers to faint and guards to draw their guns. But dispositive testimony was presented by the bank teller who said that when Mickey had threatened her he had actually said 'Give me *my* money!' not 'Give me *all your* money!' which made it clear he was not actually trying to rob the bank. So the judge dropped the bank robbery charge to a misdemeanor menacing charge and ordered him to spend thirty days in jail. And then to submit to 60 days of psychiatric observation because, well, just because he wasn't legally insane in Colorado didn't mean that he couldn't be declared legally insane in Kansas, oh no sirree!

That left him with the question of what to do with Charles Morgan and Saunders, the two young hitchhikers who had accompanied Mickey into the bank. "Well boys it appears that you are not guilty of being accessories to bank robbery, given my recent ruling with regard to Mr. Trudeau, but you are, apparently, accessories to menacing," the judge thundered from his bench. Not having had anybody before him who was guilty of this particular crime before, the judge didn't know exactly what the penalty for it should be but their court-appointed lawyer quickly put forward the idea that they plead guilty to this lesser charge with the agreement that they should be punished by time already served, and a week's worth of community service, and Charles Morgan would get his confiscated money back, which the judge accepted.

They drew their community service in an old folks home. When they got to the old folks home, one of the jobs Charles Morgan had to do was to read the bingo numbers that were drawn at the afternoon bingo games because the old folks had such poor eyesight.

One of the crabby old lady bingo players there, who almost never won, hated the way he spoke. She started to yell at him. "Where'd ya' learn to speak like that? That accent of yours is horrible! We don't need you here! What are you doing here anyway? You must have done something really, *really* wrong to be sent here!" she cackled malevolently like one of the witches in the opening scene of *Macbeth*.

Her criticisms, and the criticisms of her friends who piled onto the amusement of abusing the young juvenile 'delinquent' left Charles Morgan in tears. One day he couldn't stand it anymore and left the bingo table and went to see his friend Saunders who was working washing dishes in the kitchen.

"Saunders what will I do? They hate me out there!"

Saunders didn't appear to be listening. He was busy checking the temperature of the big tub of hot, sudsy water in front of him with a pocket thermometer. "Exactly 142.5 degrees Fahrenheit! Perfect dish washing temperature!" He beamed and thrust his hands beneath the suds to fish out one of the submerged kitchen implements that needed washing.

"Saunders!"

"Oh, sorry! Well, they probably don't all hate you. Go on out there and try again." Saunders started scrubbing a big pot that was used to boil spaghetti for the old folks.

Charles Morgan dried his eyes, and went back out to the cafeteria which was filled with tables and people playing bingo and saw that somebody else was reading the numbers. As he did so, he passed an old man, wearing all black clothes, sitting in a corner holding a book. The man was blind, but he heard Charles Morgan's footsteps passing close by and so spoke to him.

"Excuse me! Excuse me there!" he said, holding the book out toward where he thought Charles Morgan was. "Might you read to me a little bit?"

Charles Morgan took the book from him and examined the dusty cover. It was Samuel Taylor Coleridge's *"Rhyme of the Ancient Mariner"*.

"Ah, okay," he said, not too terribly eager to return to the bingo game. He opened up the book and started reading.

"Water water everywhere, nor any drop to drink..."

"My, you have a lovely voice," said the old blind man, whose hearing was especially acute. "So clear, so strong, so sweet. Haven't I heard it before?"

"Oh, I don't know," said Charles Morgan, not ready to remind anyone that a half an hour ago he had been reading bingo numbers at the other end of the room amidst the hoots and catcalls of a crabby old lady and her sycophantish friends who claimed they hated his voice.

"Well, it sounds familiar. Go on, read some more. They don't have many braille books around here that I can read," the old man said humbly. So Charles Morgan read to him for twenty minutes or so, and got to really like the poem. The old man sat silently, enraptured. He had not heard it before, and Charles Morgan had not read it before, and it was a good poem, so they both enjoyed it. After he was finished, the blind man said, "You read very well. May I ask, who you are? You sound very young."

"I'm Charles Morgan Prendergast," said Charles Morgan. "I broke the law, or rather I didn't really break the law, but I couldn't convince the judge of that, so I ended up here to quote 'pay my debt to society'. I'm doing community service."

"Oh, I see. Hold out your arm," the old man said. "Let me feel of it."

So Charles Morgan held out his arm and the old man took it in both of his hands and felt all over it, in that slow and deliberate way that blind people have of feeling things

"There's isn't a wrinkle anywhere. Your skin is smooth and supple. Good muscle tone. No flacidity. Yet not too big and muscled either. You couldn't be more than twenty-one."

"Nineteen," said Charles Morgan, impressed that the old blind man had been so accurate.

The old man bowed his head and paused while thinking. "What is it you like to do when you're not doing community service in an old folks home," he asked.

"Do?" He thought for a moment. Suddenly, he felt he could trust this very old blind man who was sitting in the corner of the room all by himself with his secret. They had, after all, just shared the experience of reading one of the most beautiful poems ever written together. "Well, you might not believe it, but I like to do yard work in the nude. The more I do it, the better I feel. And I like teaching other people how to do it, too."

You don't say," said the blind man. He seemed to accept the idea naturally, as naturally as a bee gathers pollen."Well, I have a daughter who likes to walk around without any clothes on, too. She lives out in California, in a nudist colony. But they don't call them nudist colonies anymore. They are called 'naturist communities'. Whether she likes to garden in the nude, I don't know. You might go out and ask her, though. You must realize, however, before you make the trip that she is blind, like me. That is one of the reasons she likes to go around without any clothes on. It saves her the trouble of coordinating the colors of her clothes. I have solved that problem in a different way. As you can see. I wear only black." His hand indicated his all black clothes, black shirt, black pants, black socks, and black sneakers, with a slight wave. "Black clothes are all I have in my closet and in my drawers so I can't help but pick out things that match."

The thought that there might be someone else in the world who liked to garden in the nude intrigued Charles Morgan beyond bounds. Charles Morgan was suddenly whipped up to the point of personal interest that Uncle Winkle felt when he observed the lobsters in the *Shop and Go!* He resolved right there on the spot to go out and visit the old man's daughter and see what life was like in a genuine, honest-to-goodness naturist community. For the next fifteen or twenty minutes he talked to the old man about his life and about his daughter, where she lived, how long she had been there, how many times she phoned to say hello every month, about how hard it was to be blind, what kind of dreams he had, who he had voted for in life, what had happened to his wife, etc. Things like that. A really nice conversation. Completely honest and open. Then Saunders came out of the kitchen, wiping his hands on his white dishwasher's apron, which he was taking off, since it was time to go.

As luck would have it, that was their last day of their community service. The next day they checked out of their hotel room early and started towards the rushing car sounds of the Interstate.

"Saunders I don't think I'm going to be hitching back East with you anymore."

"Huh?" said Saunders, surprised.

"I'm going to head out to California, to see Marty's daughter." Marty had been the old, blind man with whom he had felt a deep connection.

"Oh," said Saunders, a little disappointed. "Suit yourself."

"Here's some money for you to make the trip back home," said Charles Morgan reaching into his back and pulling out two hundred bucks in twenties. That ought to get you there, don't you think?" Saunders rapidly did a calculation of all the expenses he would meet along the way home.. $1.47 for a 22 oz. Mountain Dew at Seven-Eleven this afternoon,.$3.43 for a hot dog...$15.90 for sharing fuel....yeah, that'll do. I'll pay you back when I get back home."

"Don't worry Saunders. You don't need to. You're a great friend. Taught me a lot of things, and kept me out of trouble. You have my cell phone number. Call me," he said putting his hand next to his ear with the middle fingers scrunched up and the thumb and little finger outstretched in a way that meant "telephone".

And with that Charles Morgan set off walking toward the Westbound entrance ramp to the Interstate, and Saunders headed toward the Eastbound one.

9

Charles Morgan Meets the Dominatrix

One incident of note happened to Charles Morgan on his way out to California to meet Molly, Marty's daughter. Well more than one, but you can't expect me to remember everything that happened to him. He was picked up crossing Utah by a 42 year-old elementary school lunch lady driving a Fiero. She *claimed* she was driving home after work. She invited Charles Morgan over for a veggie burger for supper, and he graciously accepted. But when they got to her house the situation quickly got out of hand, and turned from what seemed to be a normal dinner invitation into something almost completely beyond Charles Morgan's ability to handle.

You see the 42 year old elementary school lunch lady was really a 42 year-old *perverted* lunch lady, which meant that she had dreams of picking up a young, handsome lad like Charles

Morgan somewhere on the road, perhaps hitchhiking, and bringing him home to her house and locking him up in chains in her basement, making him her permanent sex slave. Yep, that was what she dreamed of and hoped on. She had converted a room in her basement into a soundproof love nest where she was going to get laid every day for the rest of her life, after she got home from work, and every day before she went to work, to make up for the two decades of her life when she had not gotten laid at all, or not very much anyway. She was not a bad person, really. She did not, for instance, kidnap any of the older, good-looking high school children to fulfill her dreams. And she had never done anything else wrong her entire life. Even getting a speeding ticket was a misdeed that had escaped her. But she knew one day she would meet someone who was perfect for her scheme, for her weird idea, someone who was old enough to 'satisfy' her, and wouldn't mind getting laid himself. And she thought she might even be doing such a person a favor since she would be providing him with free food and shelter during the period of his captivity so he wouldn't have to work for a living.

She decided she was a *dominatrix*, and had even crafted a bizarre scenario in her head, based on a few girls' magazine articles on psychology she had read, how it all made sense in Freudian, or at least quasi-Freudian terms, based on the circumstances of her nearly fatherless upbringing and the odious personality of her domineering mother, and she had convinced herself that she would never be better, would never be truly mentally healthy, unless she got a chance to express her inner desire to become a dominatrix. It was like indulging her inner child which the psychologists tell us is a healthy thing to do.

So after supper, she let Charles Morgan look through her cd collection, while she disappeared for a few moments into the bedroom. She returned in a strange costume Charles Morgan had never seen before. It might have been a Halloween costume, except it wasn't Halloween. Then she led him into her secret subterranean love nest and chained him to the bed that was there, pointing a small ladies revolver at him the whole time to make sure he obeyed. Charles Morgan, who had all of his clothes on was shocked and made very anxious by this woman who had picked him up hitch-hiking with promises of a veggie burger for supper and then took him back to her house and handcuffed him to her bed, after re-appearing with a whip wearing high heels and an outlandish black suit, brandishing a revolver.

"I am the re-incarnation of Morgan Le Fey and you are the re-incarnation of Merlin the Magician and you are going to spend the rest of your life being the prisoner of my ill-lit cave, and my sex slave,"said the deranged young lady, who was none-theless quite earnest about her intentions of ravishing Charles Morgan and keeping him there forever as her sex slave, locked to the bed by the handcuffs that she had sent away for last year using the order form in a speciality police products catalog she had found in the library, and freed only once in a while by her so he could go to to the bathroom.

"I am not the re-incarnation of Merlin the Magician!" Charles Morgan snorted. Then a scheme for freeing himself began to appear in his head. "If anybody is the re-incarnation of Merlin the Magician it is my Uncle Winkle. If you would agree to meet him you'd know instantly that I was telling the truth! I'm the re-incarnation of King Arthur, and if you must know, my father is the re-incarnation of Uther Pendragon," said the nude yard man, trying to appeal to her knowledge of important although somewhat dubious English history, the truth and actual facts of which had long since vanished in the mists of time.

This appeared to faze her. "Oh, you are?" she asked somewhat quizzically. She appeared disappointed that her unique and specific theories of her own personal re-incarnation and the facts of Charles Morgan's previous life didn't seem to pan out the way she wanted them to. If the nude yard man had said that he didn't believe in re-incarnation at all, or had said that she wasn't really the re-incarnation of Morgan Le Fey, she would have whipped him. But by sounding like he knew what he was talking about, about a subject so dear to her heart, he had her in his spell. Or, to be more specific, his *counter spell*!

"Yes, I am. Now please untie me and maybe I'll help you lure my Uncle Winkle here so that you can ravish him and keep him as a sex slave forever instead of me," pleaded the nude yard man, thinking as he spoke that he probably wasn't going to do any such thing if he was freed, but if he did, Uncle Winkle probably wouldn't mind being ravished and kept a sex slave by the crazy dominatrix much anyway, especially since the Oracle had died.

She came over and said, "If I unlock these handcuffs, you aren't going to trick me, are you?" Charles Morgan secretly crossed his the index and middle fingers of his right hand which was in his lap while she was looking at his face and then shook his head, "Of course not!" Then she unlocked the handcuffs, using a key she had around her neck. As soon as she did, Charles Morgan sprang up off the bed. "Ha! I'm not really going to help you lure my kind but gullible Uncle Winkle here to be your lousy, chained-up sex slave! I just told you that so you'd free me! Now give me that whip before you hurt somebody." He yanked the whip out of her hands. She appeared puzzled and hurt and then sat down on the edge of her bed, which just moments before had held the trophy of her life and the object of her affection and years and years of careful, clandestine planning, and then slowly, quietly started to cry. Tears of dejection started rolling down her face one after another.

Charles Morgan hated to see a grown woman cry, especially one who was crying on his account. But he was conflicted about offering her any solace. After all, she had not too long ago locked him to her bed in handcuffs, and intended to keep him chained to the bed as her sex slave for the rest of his life, with only occasional trips to the bathroom.

"There, there," he said, sitting down beside her and patting her thigh. "Don't cry, okay? I'm sorry for tricking you, really I am. But you must remember that you tricked me first. I thought I was coming to your house for a veggie burger."

For the next seven hours Charles Morgan listened to Mistress Margaret, the would be dominatrix, and self-convinced real-life re-incarnation of the probably mythical Morgan LeFey explain why she had tricked him into coming over to her house for a veggie burger. She told him her life's story, about how she had been relentlessly criticized by her mother, abused by her father before he died, ridiculed by her brother, disowned by her sister, and rejected by almost every man, or woman, she had tried to have a relationship with in an effort to explain why she had set the elaborate, illegal sex slave trap that Charles Morgan had wandered into. Once she had gotten it all off her chest, she felt a lot better. As she told her story, her blouse strap slipped off her shoulder, the corner of her blouse slipped away, and out plopped a delicious looking breast. On television they call these 'wardrobe malfunctions'. So completely absorbed in her own storytelling and making sure she got it right, that she was completely oblivious to this wardrobe malfunction. Or perhaps didn't care. But Charles Morgan noticed it and began to become more and more intrigued by the possibilities it offered. While she droned on and on about her past and why she had done what she did, it seemed to beckon to him more and more, like a siren's song, and he became less and less interested in what she was saying, and more and more interested in something else.

"Hey, you know what? Let's not worry about that," said Charles Morgan looking once again at the delicious looking right breast that had just popped out of her bodice. "Let's just have sex once to see what its like, then we can be friends afterwards, OK? I won't go to the police and tell them the whole cockamamie story about how you tried to kidnap me and make me your sex slave."

She sniffled. "Well, okay..."

I don't have to describe what happened next to the reader, do I? Needless to say, Charles Morgan stuck around for a few more days and besides having sex on an almost non-stop basis, showed the somewhat nutty lady, who was really just a little bit lonely (she wasn't bad-looking, really) how to regain her self confidence by gardening in the nude. They bought a flat of petunias together down at the Agway and planted them all around her house in freshly dug flowerbeds. The cars that drove by and saw them doing this slowed down somewhat to watch, but nobody got out of their car to take pictures or gawk or anything. Seeing Margaret (for that was her name) gardening in the nude convinced them that they had been right all along about her. She was a little bit weird, but nice. And to make her happy, Charles Morgan pretended to be her captive.

One day during this short period of Charles Morgan's pretend "captivity", Mistress Margaret came down to the basement in a bad mood. She had a folded newspaper in her hand and she sat down on a chair, the chair she liked to have Charles Morgan sit on when she pretended to whip him. Then she started complaining. "Look at that, will you?!"she said, pointing to a newspaper article that she found offensive. "That damn Pastor Seymour blaming his troubles on me!" She turned to Charles Morgan for sympathy. "Imagine that! That adulterous pastor calling me a *succubus*! Why I never! I may be a dominatrix, but I'm not a *succubus*, for heavens' sake!" She pronounced the word succubus with profound distaste.

In all her dealings, Margaret was careful to make such important distinctions, distinctions which meant a lot to her judging from the amount of energy she put into making them. She was after all a self-made woman, and she wanted to be just what she wanted to be, not something else. To wear a label that someone else had stuck on her that wasn't right? She didn't like that idea at all. Just because that person was too lazy to look up the right word? Bah!

One of her favorite authors, Mark Twain, had once said, "The difference between the right word and almost the right word is the difference between lightning and a lightning bug."And Mistress Margaret envisioned her true self as being wrapped up in bright, flashing lightning bolts, not ensconced in a cloud of measly lightning bugs, if you know what I mean. A dominatrix had power. A dominatrix had class. A dominatrix had sex because she wanted to. It was a matter of her own volition. Whereas a *succubus* was sort of like a brain dead creature who was performing the sex act without any will of its own, acting according to some dark supernatural impulse that no one could explain. Uggh! She shuddered. It gave her the creeps to even think about it. She was light years away from that. *Light years!* She spoke again: "Can't people get these things right? I mean isn't it a requirement that you have to get things right to write for a newspaper?"

Charles Morgan was unaware of the actual circumstances that had led her into this foul mood or of the actual hiring standards for newspapers so all he could say in response was, "Yeah, I think so…"

What had happened was this. Mistress Margaret had gotten seduced six months ago by the local pastor who made love to her on the altar of the church, of all places. A spontaneous act with no bad vibes involved. The altar had simply been the closest thing around at the time, and they were feeling kind of, well, rushed. That was all well and good. They had both achieved satisfaction, and feeling a little sheepish afterwards at their bawdy crime, they had taken the time to clean it up properly and spend extra effort being nice to each other and cleaning and polishing around the site of what they had figured was just a frolicsome act…well, maybe a little too frolicsome! Then they had both more or less forgotten about it. But the Pastor, Pastor Seymour was his name, had been forced to confess to this matter publicly because against the rules of chance somebody had seen the two of them doing "the beast with two backs" on the altar and had reported the incident to the authorities which in this case had been the local church council. It was unfortunate, but how could they have known that a pimply-faced homeless guy who had discovered a particular unclaimed, out-of-sight horizontal space in the choir loft of the church who crept in at odd times to sleep, had peeped over the balcony railing and seen them during the course of their being *in flagrante delicto*...or whatever the proper Latin word for being coupled on the hard marble altar of an ordained Baptist Church was... and decided to spill the beans. That was what you called bad luck. Maybe really bad luck. For the pastor, anyway. He should have been contrite, confessed his guilt, resigned his post and rode off into the wild blue yonder looking for greener pastures somewhere else, perhaps in another State, or on a missionary gig in Africa or the Caribbean. But no. Not him! He was apparently made of much weaker material than that, much weaker material than the average, run of the mill philandering pastor who is caught out and shamed in front of his flock. He blamed Margaret for the affair, calling her an evil succubus who had attempted to steal his soul with an unholy act. He publicly named her in his testimony instead of manly refusing under any circumstances to name his lady accomplice.

What kind of decent guy does that? The answer: no decent guy does that. Well, of course, by blaming Margaret he was trying to save his marriage (which truth be known was in ruins anyway, that is until this opportunity for a massive dose of wife sympathy came his way!) as well as save his salaried position at the church. But still, in the Book of Love, such things are for-bidden! The pimply faced homeless guy knew it was the pastor on the altar because he was dressed in his frock and he had seen him give a service before, albeit when he was in a more or less vertical position behind the altar rather than in a more or less horizontal position on top of the altar. But he didn't know who the woman was. He had never seen her before. She was in the clear until her faithless lover decided to spill the beans. That was why Margaret was hopping mad when she read that newspaper. And even though she was a dominatrix who had kidnapped Charles Morgan and kept him chained up in her basement as her love slave and fed him nothing but bread and water and the oc-casional veggie burger when she was feeling generous, that had nothing to do with it. She had a right to be irate about the out-rageous indiscretion of this pastor and his mis-characterization of their one-time tryst. After all, he was the one who had initi-ated it. It was absolutely prevaricating to say otherwise. And *evil succubus*? WTF? Where did that come from?

The newspaper article went on to say that the church hier-archy had investigated and ordered that the church altar be burnt since it was irreparably stained with unspeakable sin and beyond redemption. It would be sacrilegious to do otherwise. So Margaret was not only being blamed for the corruption of a well-known local pastor, and maybe breaking up his family, but also for the considerable expense of removing, burning and replacing the church's beautiful marble altar. That's why she was so agitated and had decided to come down and seek some sympathy from Charles Morgan. Well, decided is too rational a word. She instinctively knew in her heart that she wasn't the bad person that the newspaper article was making her out to be, and who better to agree with her than the wonderful man she had locked up in her basement? He could see how wonderful and kind, and how benevolent and loving she really was, couldn't he?

She had sought his solace out blindly, automatically, and inexorably like Newton's apple falling to the Earth.

Seeing Margaret in the state she was in, Charles Morgan sighed. Here was another layer to Margaret's complicated life situation that he would have to unravel before he could leave her with a clean conscience, knowing that she was going to be okay on her own without him.

So he calmed her down and got her to tell him the story of her involvement with Pastor Seymour with all its ins and outs (pardon the phrase!) including the very relevant fact that the pastor was married with three children, and that neither one of the tryst partners had noticed the homeless guy up in the choir loft, and how Margaret had just been "some broad"until he, Pastor Seymour, had named her, probably forever ruining her reputation in the community. He tried to figure out what kind of a scallywag would blame an otherwise innocent girl for his own bad luck and misadventure and use an episode like that to actually get ahead in life. It wasn't a pretty character picture. Whatever else, the guy deserved a beating. But you couldn't just go around giving a beating to everybody who deserved one, unless you were Mike Tyson, or the mafia, or the God of the Old Testament, who gave everyone a metaphorical beating, and who probably really meant it when he said "Vengeance is Mine!"because he was that jealous and vindictive and truly loved to kick ass. So some other form of punishment was called for, maybe something that would involve a little bit of time to think about. In the meantime....

Yes, in the meantime, perhaps they could play one of their little "games" Maybe that would distract Margaret from her misery.

Charles Morgan asked: "Is it alright if we play a little game, Margaret?"Margaret looked at him quizzically, and didn't answer. But she didn't say "No"

"I am just a little violet growing in a field of wildflowers and someone is coming to pick me! Mistress Margaret you must save me! Oh, please save me, Magic Margaret with your love, save me!"Charles Morgan said, trying to sound like a poor, defenseless flower.

"Of course I will save you my precious little flower, and my don't you look soft and pretty today,"said Margaret, tentatively, not sure whether she was ready to shift gears from being mad and indignant to being playful and absorbed in one of their provocative but ultimately silly role-playing games.

"Yes, I feel very soft and pretty and ready for you, Mistress..."

Suddenly the doorbell rang. That was the kind of thing Uncle Winkle the worrywart would worry about, thought Charles Morgan to himself. Hmmph! At least he hadn't been worrying about it! But it did happen. He wondered about the implications of that.

"Now who could that be?"wondered Margaret, who wasn't expecting any visitors. She ran upstairs to open the door.

Well that ruined that particular role-playing episode! The vibe was gone.

It wasn't long after, perhaps about a week or two, before Charles Morgan started to get bored with being Mistress Margaret's prisoner in the basement, pretending to be poor defenseless flowers and other crazy things. He missed raking leaves, feeling the sunshine on his body, working, seeing new sites, and meeting new people. So he decided to leave. He had boosted Margaret's self confidence, he thought, to the level where she would be okay without him and would be able to function in society without their crazy daily hank-panky. So he wrote her a letter

Dear Margaret,

I have decided to leave. I have become bored with our role playing games and want to reclaim my own life again. I don't want to hurt your feelings. We had a lot of fun together. But we both know it wasn't meant to last forever.

Good luck,

Charles Morgan

Feeling like one of the more eccentric characters from the song *"There Must Be Fifty Ways to Leave Your Lover"*, he put the letter on his pillow and picked the handcuff holding his left arm to the bed post on the 6 foot chain he had allowed Margaret to put on him. It was easy. All you needed was a paperclip for heaven's sake! Read Houdini's book or almost any book on escape acts and you'll see how it can be done. Then he grabbed his clothes and rucksack which were in a corner of the room, opened up one of the basement windows which Margaret had clumsily cardboard-ed over to prevent the neighbor's kids from accidentally seeing what was going on in the basement, and crawled out into the sunshine. Ah, it was a glorious day!

Making his way to the Interstate, Charles Morgan wondered what Mary would think about all this when he told her when he finally made up with her. *If* he finally made up with her, he reminded himself. And *if* he told her about it, which he probably wouldn't ,and probably shouldn't given how sensitive she was on issues like this one. She might take Charles Morgan's explanation the wrong way, and view the episode not as an adventure in which Charles Morgan had barely escaped with his life, and only by using his wits to their fullest extent, but as a slap in the face to her. And it wasn't a slap in the face to her. He would never slap Mary in the face. She was his best friend and always would be, even though he hadn't yet decided whether he was actually going to make up with her. So best to put that issue to rest and mull it over later, when he had time to think about it better and more fully.

Did we forget to mention that Mary and Charles Morgan were at loggerheads at this time? Well they were. A few days after making the decision at Uncle Leigh's to hitchhike around the country Charles Morgan had called Mary to explain it to her.

"You what? Decided to hitchhike around the country instead of coming home to be with me? Well I never! What are you, crazy? Don't you ever call me again," she said. And then she hung up on him. He describes the incident with more detail in his *Memoirs*, but that's more or less the way it went down. Obviously she didn't really mean what she said about not calling her again, and they both knew that, but that's what the situation was when Charles Morgan left Margaret's. So we can understand why our hero was a bit diffident and maybe a little circumspect about that relationship.

After thinking about his strategy some more, Charles Morgan decided it really wasn't right to leave Mistress Margaret this way. He was about halfway to the Interstate entrance ramp on the outskirts of town when he decided to turn back and tell her he was leaving. He got back to the house and crept in through the still open basement window. Then he tore up the note and laid back on the bed staring at the ceiling.

Margaret came home a few hours later. "Hi Honey," she said descending the basement stairs. "Hi Margaret," Charles Morgan said. And then he proceeded to tell her how he had loosened his handcuffs, written her a note, opened up the basement window and walked toward the Interstate to take off without saying goodbye like one of the more eccentric, unmentioned characters in *50 Ways to Leave Your Lover* and then had decided to come back and tell her he was leaving after all because he felt bad about it. She listened intently, looking away from him, (a thousand yards away, it seemed to him!) and didn't react much after he had finished. "Anyway, I felt guilty. I couldn't leave you that way."

Somehow she seemed to understand that her days of wholesome frolicking around in the basement as the reincarnation of the probably mythical Morgan Le Fey had reached a natural conclusion. "You know what darling, I don't blame you one bit. This basement *can* get a little stuffy. You need time to breathe and to think. Go on out into that brave new world out there and see what you can do to make it a better place. And remember me and all the good times we've had together. In the meantime, let me fix you a veggie burger. We'll have some dinner, watch the news, sleep together maybe and then you can leave in the morning. How does that sound? "

"That sounds good. Except could you make it pancakes instead of a veggie burger?" asked Charles Morgan.

You see, besides being a would be dominatrix, Margaret was also a really good novelty pancake maker. She could make heart-shaped pancakes, pancakes with people's initial's on them, pancakes with blueberries arranged in smiley faces on them, cantaloupe pancakes, pancakes with raspberry jelly and Jimmy Dean sausages inside them and all sorts of other delicious kinds of pancakes that you wouldn't find on the IHOP menu even if you turned it over three or four times to make sure you weren't missing anything. She was a veritable Pancake Queen and the only reason she didn't enter her pancakes in a baking contest was because the thought of all that notoriety and rubbing shoulders with all those plain ordinary moms and cheerful house makers scared her to death. She was a very private person and if they started asking questions about what she did, well, she was afraid her answers wouldn't satisfy them very much and they would come hunting for more information to feed the gossip grapevine. And she didn't want that at all! Because she was not only a private person but a private person with a secret life! But she did like to make novelty pancakes, though. It showed you cared about life. And it was a neat thing to do.

"Sure!" she replied.

So she made apple cinnamon pancakes, with lots of apples and lots of cinnamon in them, and on the outside they had dripped on to them some extra drools of batter which spelled out the message "I Love You, CM! "

Wow! You see how people can change? Don't ever think that they can't! Especially when in close contact with the alembic powers of Charles Morgan Prendergast.

I don't have to describe what happened the next morning to the reader, do I? When they parted, they were the best of friends and he promised to email her when he got to his destination to let her know how he was doing. She let him off at a good entrance ramp to the Interstate and then took off in her Fiero, waving merrily.

10

Charles Morgan Meets the Naturists

When Charles Morgan got to the naturist community in Big Sur, California to visit blind Molly, two guys from Northampton, Massachusetts were there visiting a friend. They were two of the foremost experts on permaculture and sustainable agriculture in the United States. Their friend had been a professor at Colgate University, and then had gone out to a California think tank, the California Rural Lands Institute, to raise money for sustainable agriculture programs. They were out there visiting him and had stopped by the naturist community for a few days to check it out.

These two authors and professional activists knew things about gardening that Charles Morgan didn't have any idea about. Charles Morgan just knew about gardening from what Uncle Leigh had taught him, and what he had taught himself by observation, and by reading a few gardening magazines. But these two guys were among the world's top experts in the way gardening was evolving on a world scale. And they were there at the naturist community, totally relaxed and approachable. So you can imagine when he got there that Charles Morgan was head over heels delighted to listen to them talk, sitting around the campfire in the evenings during the community sing-alongs.

If you were one of the millions of people who had a home garden, and who were considering becoming more self sufficient and energy secure, then you wanted to listen to these two fellows because they had all sorts of ideas and facts brimming out of their heads that you could profit from. Biodiesel? They could tell you what the best kind of oil seeds were and where to find the best screw presses to extract the oil. Regenerative farming? They knew all about that. Urban gardens? They had written three papers on them. Name a subject in gardening and they knew all about it, from planting Echinacea to harvesting sunflower seeds.

If you were committed to finding solutions to reducing the country's carbon footprint, energy conservation, energy efficiency planning, or renewable technologies, they were the people to listen to. It was a great time to be alive and gardening, according to what they had to say. There was a beautiful future coming. Edible landscaping, regenerative farming, carbon-neutral energy production, 'permaculture', were all the rage. All the right people were behind them. Edible forest gardens, edible urban gardens, vertical building yardens, they were the New Frontier for humanity. Most people didn't think about these things. But these two guys from Northhampton did. And they shouted them from the rooftop!. A lot of people were into artificial intelligence (AI), fusion energy, cryptocurrencies, and other things, but these two guys made modern gardening sound like the coolest thing happening.

It was really lucky that they were there when Charles Morgan showed up. He became an instant disciple. Here is part of what he learned.

Permaculture? Permaculture is a term that was coined in 1978 by Bill Mollison and David Holmgren, two Australians. It has three components: a vision for a human society living in harmony with Nature, a design system to help us create that vision (and integrate ecological design principles into all aspects of human society, from food production to accounting, to whatever else you can think of that humans do), and a global network of people who are committed to that vision.

Why? People are redoing how they live in response to peak oil, and energy descent. They are redoing their lives in ways which make sense. They are turning away from big corporations and what they have to offer. They are trying to prepare for a future without corporations in it. The Association to Study Peak Oil says we have hit the Hubbert Curve peak already, or will soon if we haven't already. Population, fertilizer use, water use, and other things are also exponentially peaking. Ecological systems cannot sustain exponential growth like that for very long. What permaculture is all about is how to creatively descend from that peak of energy use. The three scenarios are: (1) a continuation of exponential growth, which most people regard as a techno-fantasy, (2) a crash of civilization, or (3) a long, sustainable period of proper earth stewardship with green-tech stability, photovoltaics, wind power, etc.

How? How do we gracefully and ethically descend? The idea of a descent from growth seems like the wrong idea in our culture but really it's the most logical thing to do. We have to descend to some lower level of energy use because we cannot sustain the present high rate of energy consumption meeting all our needs. At the same time we must regenerate the health of the ecosystem, because lets face it, we have destroyed much of the earth's ecosystem, including thousands of unique species, with likely more catastrophic extinction events on the way.

Permaculture regenerative design is about how to do that, i.e., regenerate our ecosystems in a human cultural context so that we have healthy ecosystems in our own backyard and everybody's else's backyard, too. Sustainability teachers, ecological designers, and organic gardeners are committed to creating a more vital and beautiful future, regenerative farming. Our food, our homes, and the way they intersect is called 'permaculture' when they all come together in just the right way.

Where? A reclaimed lot in downtown Holyoke. A community farm in Amherst. In 14 years seven more gardens and two special purpose gardens focused on youth in Pittsfield. Ten gardens up and running reclaimed from abandoned or decrepit lots in the town all revolving around this idea of building community and personal stability and resilience through projects related to agriculture. The environment and individual health expand from simple community gardens where people are growing produce for themselves, providing an incubator for entrepreneurs who start small farm businesses but primarily cater to culturally appropriate and difficult-to-find foods. The low income people who lived there broke it up into 1/8 and 1/4 acre lots and gave people an opportunity to grow their own food. In one year they realized there was way more demand than they could accommodate on those 4 acres. Or take the 26 acres owned by a Connecticut convent. Since 2010 they have supported 15 small farm businesses for 5 years. They have festivals every fall, pig roasts every Saturday; and all kinds of really exciting cultural activities growing out of that in terms of social and business partnerships

One of the principles of permaculture is that we try to functionally interconnect different design elements. The inherent yield of one type of design element meets the inherent needs of another. So the pig farmers are happy to see the pig roasts.

Periodic droughts are happening more often and water restrictions are becoming more common, in all parts of the country. They were close to having to shut down the city of Atlanta's water recently. Climate disruption means more heavy rainfalls and longer, more intense droughts. Which seems paradoxical but when the storms come they are likely to be big storms with a lot of rain which will run off and cause floods and then long periods between the storms when it will get dry. So we need to be designing for both drought and flood at the same time. We need to take that flood water and get it in the ground to store it and replenish the nation's hard-hit aquifers. We need to reduce the amount of drought-making pavement! For years engineers learned to channelize water and get it into the rivers and out to sea. Those urban runoff waters carry pollutants and affect fisheries adversely. People are digging up their asphalt driveways with sledgehammers and saws and replanting that area in gardens, growing fruits and berries and vegetables and forage for their chickens.

The plants are evapo-transpirating the water away whereas the asphalt, besides channelizing the water, retains heat so by getting rid of it, you reduce the urban "heat island" effect and you reduce your need for air conditioning, too. In fact, you can reduce heating and cooling energy demands by up to 1/3rd depending on what you do, just by using landscaping! And if you think carefully about the plant species you're using, you can get additional yields of food, medicine, useful fibers, and forage for animals. It all works together.

We mimic the structure and function of natural ecosystems in order to gain a whole host of benefits. By having multiple layers of vegetation, tree branches in the canopy, under-story trees, and shrubs, herbs, vines, and roots near the ground, we can actually get much higher productivity in every locale, and a much higher yield because we have plants at different levels which are adapted to different amounts of sunlight that are giving us the different products. Fruits and nuts need a lot of sun. But in the shade you can grow a lot of greens and medicinals, gooseberries and currants There is no reduction in yield for 40% shade for red currants, for instance. Strawberries for the daquiri, mint for the julep....sun and shade.

As the fathers of permaculture said, we seek to recreate the garden of Eden, and why not? All that it's going to take is human ingenuity, and the will to do it. If we can put a man on the moon, why not create a new garden of Eden on Earth? Food security and self maintaining ecosystems are the wave of the future!

So how do we reduce the work we have to do by proper design of the system? By planting species that enrich the subsoil so you don't need fertilizers! Nitrogen is the key thing because most nitrogen fertilizer right now comes from natural gas. People are planting more gardens. There's a strong, steady increase in gardening that is spiking so we have more work than we can do.

People are tearing up their lawns and putting in gardens There's 30 million acres of lawn in the United States. 12% of the continental U.S. is lawns which use 2-3 times more water than a fruit tree or shrub. The recession gardens are kind of like the old victory gardens they had in WWII. The naysayers say 'So what! People are planting gardens!" Well, in 1943 the USDA launched a campaign and victory gardens produced 40% of the food grown in the country. In Russia today 40% of their produce is produced on small, 1/4 acres lots, and so small plots can make a really meaningful contribution. And if edible landscapes are designed to mimic natural ecosystems then we can provide water cleaning and habitats for insects and cooling and reflect more sunlight to battle global warming.

But it's the people connection that's the most transformative aspect of this new movement. Before we were disconnected from each other and the environment, but by getting out there and gardening with others and watching what is happening we can rebuild those connections.

"Wow," said Charles Morgan. "That's a lot to do and think about!" When he shared what he was doing in the outside world, everybody loved that, too. Wow! Was he brave. They weren't afraid to garden in the nude on the grounds of the naturist community, but to do it outside in the real world? That took real courage!

Luckily for him, the first day he got there, Molly invited him to share her yurt with her. Keeping house with a blind girl was... different. Somehow she could tell what his mood was without seeing the expression on his face.

One day Charles Morgan decided to surprise her. "I bought a collection of Coleridge's poems, Molly. Your dad and I read his *The Rhyme of the Ancient Mariner* together and I thought you'd enjoy it if we read some of his other poems," he said to Molly one night in her comfortable yurt where they had a fire cackling because the weather was kind of chilly.

"OK," she said.

"This one is called *Kubla Khan*. It goes like this..."

"In Xanadu did Kubla Khan

A stately pleasure-dome decree:

Where Alph, the sacred river, ran

Through caverns measureless to man

Down to a sunless sea.

So twice five miles of fertile ground

With walls and towers were girdled round;

And there were gardens bright with sinuous rills,

Where blossomed many an incense-bearing tree;

And here were forests ancient as the hills,

Enfolding sunny spots of greenery...."

"Oh, I can see that, Charles! It's lovely. I can see it, the underground river, the caverns, the gardens, the forests and the sunny spots of greenery. I can see it all!" she exclaimed looking at all the beautiful images in her mind that the poem had evoked. It seemed that Charles Morgan's voice had the power to allow her to see things like forests, and sunshine and the color green. Of course she had been in forests so she knew what they felt like. And she had felt sunshine on her face and nude body many times so she knew what "sunshine" felt like too. But the color green? Ah, well... Maybe she knew it was supposed to be the color associated with soft green growing plants which she could feel with her hands and the delicious-feeling grass when she walked barefoot, or laid down on it. Or maybe mind-melding powers ran in the poem reader's family. Who knows? But on that night Molly the blind naturist girl claimed she could see the color green.

One day at the naturist community CM discovered how to untangle an extension cord. The members wanted to set up a big-screen tv by the campfire that night so they could watch a movie. And they needed a 100 ft extension cord to plug into an outlet in the nearest cabin. But the one they had was all tangled up and it was Charles Morgan's job to untangle it. Normally a person starts at one end or the other and then works their way to the other end. But that takes forever which is why nobody ever wants to be bothered. CM, given the job of untangling the only old, jumbled-up extension cord they could find, found a way to start in the middle and untangle the loops within the loops. He discovered that by doing so you could untangle a long extension cord in about 1/5th of the time that starting at one end and working your way to the other end took. All you had to do was undo the loops within the loops and then, eventually, the ends fell away clean. Oh, maybe there were one or two knots that according to the rules of topology were still left as actual knots after doing this, but undoing them was a snap because there remained so few of them and because each one fell into its own separate place like beads on the line of an abacus.

If he ever published a book, he would tell people about this discovery of his for free so that millions of people, even people he never met, could untangle 100' or 150' extension cords that looked hopeless, and save many hours of precious time. That was his idea. That was how kindly he thought about people, even people he didn't know. He instinctively wanted to help people, even if he didn't know them, or didn't 'get anything out of it'. That was just the way he was. That was the way he was when he was showing people how to garden in the nude, too. He believed that he was helping them. Spiritually, of course. But also physically, for he knew that people who gardened in the nude drastically improved their health.

While he was there at that little ecological oasis in the woods, he learned new words from the naturists like "clothing optional", and "textile beach", and "top free", instead of "topless". One of their sacred screeds proudly listed 217 different things about nudity that you probably didn't know. He found out, for instance, that if an ordinary clothed person met a nude man walking in the woods, their opinion of the experience would be five times more positive than if they had encountered a hunter with his or her clothes on. That result was in one of the polls the naturists had conducted. He found out that there was nothing in the Bible that said it was wrong to go around in the nude. He learned that children in primitive tribes who are surrounded by nudity of all types suffer no ill effects. Learning these things made him believe even more strongly in the virtue of naked yard work.

The women of the Happy Acres naturist community were of a fiercely independent, feisty variety, who occasionally slapped their children and their men when they did something wrong, didn't shave their legs or their armpits very often, weren't afraid to breast-feed their babies in public, and avoided the plastic smells like those found inside Walmart toy departments, or new cars, or water bottles like the plague. They were acutely aware of toxics, especially toxics fashioned by the military industrial complex and consumer America. They wre the type of women who could love and be loved by a single man or a tribe. They were often exquisitely beautiful, and if you met a group of them you would feel like you had met a band of princesses traveling for a rainbow gathering. The men were all good, hardworking, honest, solid fellows of strong character who you could depend on. It was all in all a pretty good place to be, and a good place to learn about naturism, gardening, and gardening in the nude. Clothing optional gardening they called it. A sunhat, an open cotton shirt, and the bottom half of a bikini was considered well dressed. To guard against mosquitoes they did put some clothes on when they sat around the campfire at night. Sometimes they did anyway.

One night they were sitting around the campfire and telling stories and discussing philosophical questions as people do when they get together. One question that came up was whether all evil in society stemmed from the use of clothes. There were those who advocated that point of view in the naturist camp, just like there were those in the field of economics who declaimed that all evil stemmed from the use of locks, since locks guaranteed a way to protect private property and made the dubious private property system inevitable. The evening campfire at the California naturist community was a somewhat different forum than academia, but there was just as much passion on both sides of the debate, and just as many winning arguments on either side, so that the uncommitted who sat around the campfire and listened were swayed first one way and then the other.

One of the doubters of this presumed truth, Josh Ande_____, snorted. "Oh things were just so great back in the state of nature weren't they. They didn't starve, and freeze their buns off and get sick with all sorts of nasty germs that modern science has protected us from now, did they? And all the fruits of civilization should just be cast aside in favor of a complete return to Nature? All our machines thrown into the ocean to rust, so we can all just prance around without any clothes on for the rest of of our lives, instead of just on holidays and weekends in some sort of perpetual Garden of Eden Ver. 2.0? Not! Answer me one question, will you? How did they clip their nails in the Garden of Eden? Before nail clippers or scissors? Huh? You tell me that? How in the heck did they clip their nails without nail clippers or scissors, and prevent them from growing way too long and ripping off by accident without nail clippers or scissors?"

The members of the campfire council all stared off into space wondering just how people did clip their nails back then.

Some looked into the fire and some looked out into the darkness. They honestly didn't know. And it seemed like an important question, too. Everybody knew how painful a torn fingernail or toenail could be. And everybody knew that the only way you could prevent them was to keep your nails trimmed. Scissors certainly hadn't been around forever, and nail clippers even less long. How had they done it? 'Did they have scissors during the time of Christ?' some of them wondered to themselves, the "time of Christ" being for many people a reference point of the unimaginably distant human past, lost forever in the mists of Time, even though it wasn't really THAT long ago.

They had never confronted this thorny question of the history of personal grooming before. But they had just assumed that…. Well, what had they assumed? To a person, they had never really contemplated the question at all before! Soon they started smiling at each other around the campfire. They were all genuinely dumbfounded. Josh had scored a point! They knew that Josh wasn't a True Believer. He was just a weekend person, there for an occasional thrill. He wasn't a core member of the community, and nobody liked to see him score points like this because his views were so often at odds with the mainstream camp viewpoints. But this time, they had to hand it to him, he had scored a point. How the heck *did* people trim their nails before scissors were invented? Surely there must have been some way to do it… but if there hadn't been…think about the agony all those poor people had to suffer through with all those countless, painful ripped finger and toenails! Several of them shuddered, just thinking about it. Maybe life in the state of nature wasn't so great after all!

Josh didn't like to be rude. But he didn't let his weekend preference for clothing optional environments cloud his judgment about the actual utility of civilization and technology, including clothes and the technology of the personal grooming industry.

Now the other members of the community could see where he was coming from. He was coming from a tradition of intellectual honesty. He was coming from the Socratic tradition, the viewpoint that Truth, and telling the Truth was the most important thing of all, above even friendship.

No one had an answer to Josh's question so that the contentious conversation regarding the evil of clothes just sort of faded away into a mildly embarrassing silence, and in its place someone picked up a guitar and began singing a renaissance madrigal. Others joined in and soon everyone was singing joyfully around the campfire like it was a YMCA camp back in the 1960's, or something.

Regardless of the ultimate philosophical conclusion about the use of clothes, there really was something marvelous and majestic about being able to walk around in the nude all the time at the naturist community. But after about three weeks of being there, Charles Morgan was beginning to feel restless. He didn't want to just walk around in the nude all the time. He only wanted to do it when he was gardening. That was enough for him. Gardening was a big part of his life, but it wasn't the only part. He liked to do other things as well, like go to the movies, ride on trains, and hitchhike. He certainly couldn't imagine hitchhiking without any clothes on. And so he thought about leaving and what he wanted to do next. He decided to go into town to get some maps. So he went to the second hand book store in town and bought some old gas station maps of Idaho and a few other states that he wanted to visit. Then he stopped by the local pub, Gary's Wishbone, for a cold beer because it was a hot day and the idea of a refreshment appealed to him.

He walked up to the bar, ordered and paid for a Heineken and took a long cool drink. Ahh! That hit the spot! He smacked his lips savoring the taste. Then he spread his map out on the worn, zinc counter of the bar and began to study it, trying to decide what the best way was to get to Sun Valley.

The conversation resumed between the man sitting next to him at the bar and the bartender. The man sitting at the bar next to him had a dark blue windbreaker on that had the big yellow letters "FBI" printed on the back.

"...and let me tell you something else about those naturists," said the man with the FBI windbreaker on who looked a lot like a younger version of Archie Bunker.

"Their purpose is not just to build one little enclave, one isolated little sanctuary, where they can take their clothes off. Oh no siree! They have grander designs than that. They want to build a whole nationwide network of completely independent, self-supporting tax-free sanctuaries where they can take their clothes off and go back to nature. And then they are going to push their naturist philosophy on the rest of us. They have no intention of keeping to themselves and minding their own business. Oh, no! Their purpose is to propagandize, and evangelize!"

The bartender asked, "So? What's the matter with that? What's at risk if they do?"

"What's at risk?"asked the man who was wearing the FBI windbreaker, surprised that anyone would even contemplate asking that question. "Why what's at risk is our very way of life! Not just our American way of life, but the way of life of all nations. Civilization itself. The 30 year mortgage, the seven year car loan, the quick trip down to the convenience store to buy a pack of smokes, buying a guy a drink at the bar because you like him, changing into a suit and tie for a dinner date, showing up for your wedding in a wedding gown and tuxedo. It's all at risk if the naturists have their way! Nothing will be hidden anymore. It will all be hanging out there in the open for everybody to see. Nobody will have any secrets anymore, not if we live the way *they* want us to live, and if its one thing I know, if there's one thing I've learned in the FBI, its that people LOVE their secrets. They *have* to have them. It's like trying to breathe without air. Forget about whether the boss wears a toupee, or if the boss is a female whether she wears pads to make her boobs look bigger, we're talking about all sorts of secrets here, secrets of the kind that clothing and all that clothing represents only hide metaphorically. Those secrets and others like them are what separate the human race from all other animals, and from chaos and anarchy. And those are the secrets we FBI guys are sworn to protect! A Nation needs its secrets. It will positively collapse without them." He lifted his glass and drained the last swig of Johnny Walker Black that it contained, absolutely, positively convinced that what he had just said was the truth.

He continued. "And so to combat this growing naturist *menace*, we have plans to infiltrate and disrupt this repugnant movement. We will spare no effort at identifying who the key members are and keeping track of them, their movements, their phone calls, their letters, their magazine subscriptions, the books they read, and their library records. We will keep them in our crosshairs until we have detailed profiles of their characters and psychologies, detailed and sufficient enough to know whether an individual will stop for a donut in the morning or an egg

McMuffin. We have put in place vast resources for this effort and there are numerous on-going operations at the present time, most of which are classified and cannot be divulged without draconian legal penalties and stiff fines, but mark my words, they exist!"

Then he looked in Charles Morgan's direction to see if he'd been listening. Suddenly his eyes narrowed and he looked at Charles Morgan with newfound interest. He recognized him from a surveillance picture that had been contained in a report he had read on the Happy Acres naturist community. "Hey, I know you! You're Charles Morgan Prendergast! The Nude Yardman!"

"Yes?"

You really are a winner, aren't you? Trying to destabilize the good ole USA with all your naked yardman *sturm* and *drang*.

"I haven't broken any federal laws," replied Charles Morgan, wishing the guy would leave him alone. What had happened to the quality of FBI agents these days, anyway? Where were the paragons of exemplary behavior he remembered? The clever cool agents like Mulder and Scully in the *X Files*?

"Oh maybe you did. And maybe you didn't. Whether we can prove it one way or another doesn't matter. You think your old George Stalin had one over on us?" asked the FBI man, who was more than slightly tipsy.

"Joseph," said Charles Morgan

"What?"

"I hate to upset your apple cart, but his name was *Joseph* Stalin. His first name was Joseph."

"George! Joseph! What does it matter. You think he had one over on us when he said, *"Don't worry about the crime. Just give us the man. We'll figure out a crime."* Ha! That ain't nothing compared to what we got! Ever hear of the Patriot Act? And its extensions? We can hold you for an unlimited amount of time on just the mere suspicion of your being an agent of a foreign power. And we don't need to tell anybody we got you, neither! And boy, that's just what I'm gonna do!" He pulled a pair of handcuffs out of his pocket, they appeared as if by magic, and clinked them down on Charles Morgan's left wrist which was holding a green Heineken bottle which was only half finished. But before he could get them locked onto it, Charles Morgan whipped his arm back and inadvertently splashed some of the beer from the bottle in the drunk agents eyes which made him lose his vision momentarily. Then Charles Morgan calmly placed the bottle down on the bar, picked up his map, and walked out of the bar while the agent was reaching for a napkin to wipe his eyes dry.

"Did you see that," the Agent asked the bartender.

"See what?" the bartender asked.

"That little whippersnapper threw beer in my eyes!"

"Buddy, you've had too much to drink. I didn't see nuthin' of the sort. Why don't we settle up."

While Charles Morgan walked slowly back to the naturist community, the agent spluttered nonsense phrases as drunk people do, searching unsuccessfully for the money in his pockets to pay his bar bill. He eventually filed a FR-25 field report on the incident, but it went no further than the local field office. His supervisor didn't really believe he had been lucky enough to run into Charles Morgan Prendergast in a random bar in Big

Sur, California and have his attempt to handcuff him (without probable cause) thwarted by a chance splash of beer in his eyes. They thought he was telling fairy tales. That was the expression the FBI bureaucrats had for reports that came in from the field that the supervisors found unreliable.

So for better or worse the drunken, garrulous FBI man didn't arrest Charles Morgan that day on bogus, trumped up charges that would have met with the smiling approval of George, er Joseph Stalin.

11

Charles Morgan is Filled With a Terrible Resolve

Charles Morgan did not take kindly to learning about the government's monitoring of naturists in the United States. In fact, it made him mad as hell. In response, he vowed to redouble his efforts to teach nude yard working to the masses. That was what made him want to leave the safe confines of the Happy Acres naturist community sooner than he had planned. His decision was tied in with contemplations of what had happened to his dad.

During the four long years of his father's time in jail, Charles Morgan had had a long time to contemplate the philosophies of the possible represented by his father, and the philosophies of the impossible, represented, for lack of any other good person on a handy basis, Uncle Winkle. His father was all positive, had lots of faith in god, and believed in people. Uncle Winkle was a nethering nabob of negativism, an atheist, and thought people were not to be trusted most of the time. The funny thing was, his dad, with his good vibes and positive energy was in jail while his Uncle Winkle, a nethering nabob of negativism (for the most part) was free as a bird

He struggled in the attempt to reconcile what happened to his father in his mind. The dried flowers that his father was originally arrested for were originally fresh flowers, weren't they, that the Almighty God put on the earth? How could you be arrested for possessing or "trafficking" in what God had already put on the earth, especially flowers? It didn't make sense. It was one of those laws with a completely obscure origin. That fact that his father had been arrested for trafficking in the obviously innocuous dried flowers had allowed him a glimpse beneath the surface of the *seemingly* well-ordered world around him. It *appeared* to be benignly structured by law, but really it was filled with senselessness and irrationality underneath that thin veneer of civility. Such a vision filled him with dread for it reeked of doom. And if he became melancholy at times after his father's arrest and after his mother left him, it was because this vision of the world would return to haunt him at times. It would grip him with its dark power, filling him with uncontrollable paroxysms of grief and despair. Sometimes he would wake up in a cold sweat having had a nightmare about it. It wasn't merely hypothetical this dark power, rooted in mindlessness and irrationality. It was very real and dangerous, for it had taken his loving father away from him, and then, by a knock on effect, his mother, too.

It was only when he took off all his clothes and did yard work in the nude that he felt he was able to defeat this dark power, and to put it in its place for all time. Then, communing with nature, he felt connected with all the wonderful, good things in the world, all the things that made sense and always would, as if invisible tendrils emanated from each atom in his body to all of them. Then he was a beautiful, shining, and loving creation of the Universe, part of a mindful unfolding that couldn't be stopped. The prohibition against nudity, and especially nudity when doing yard work, was one of those laws that simply didn't make sense and never would. It was simply ass-backwards crazy.

How could it be against the law to garden in the nude when it made you so much more productive and felt so good? It was not only good for your body, it was also good for your soul, for by doing it you were casting off all those unhealthy, stultifying social conventions that didn't make sense, and declaring to the world that you were not going to be limited by them anymore, and that you were going to live your life according to higher principles. There was something alembic and revolutionary about it too, the statement you were making, because everybody could see how easy it was to do. You didn't need money or power to do it. You only had to have a little bit of courage which everybody had. And so there was nobody who could stop you if you wanted to do it. And the more people did it, the easier it became. So Charles Morgan figured he was doing the right thing in so many ways by teaching people how to do yardwork in the nude.

Really, when you carefully considered it, it was a very strange and abnormal thing to teach young children to be ashamed and embarrassed about their nudity. It was completely unnatural. They were born into the world nude. That was an unmistakable fact about their lives which no one could have any doubts about. So that teaching them to be ashamed and embarrassed about their own nudity as they grew older, for instance scolding them when they didn't have any clothes on in front of people, was in effect teaching them to be ashamed and embarrassed about their own selves and individual identity on the most basic level, a form of learned self-hatred that was akin to the guilt trip of original sin. As such it could be conceived of as an entirely unnecessary, self-serving and malevolent conspiracy designed to put members of the human race who believed in it at a distinct disadvantage from the get go. In essence, the widespread and longstanding belief that it was necessary for people to wear clothes was a case of a fatuous, distorted belief system taking hold and then being inherited by each new generation on a massive, structural level, a fooling of the people that had no equal in History. It was doomed to die an ignominious death because it was founded on untruth. The use of clothes in effect was pure propaganda promulgated under the undue influence and control of the clucking lips of smug moralists, fashion designers, clothiers and others who were getting rich by exploiting the materialistic, Ahrimanic weaknesses of human beings. This latter group of people were closely linked with that other group of people who didn't believe in global warming, thought pollution was good, and started wars in order to get rich. Thus metaphysically, one *could* actually equate the use of clothes with evil, and not be very far off the mark. Remember, if you will, that was only after Adam and Eve had eaten of the forbidden fruit that they became ashamed of their own nudity.

Nude yard work was the answer to so many of the world's vexing problems, Charles Morgan thought. For instance, wouldn't those seething hordes in the middle east soon stop killing each other if they didn't have any clothes on and were gardening? How could you carry a gun without any clothes on? And nudity automatically eliminated the particularly vexatious problem of the suicide bomber. Nobody could carry around 4 pounds of C4, 20 pounds of ball bearings, and a detonator if they didn't have any clothes on! Or if you did have them strapped to your body everybody would see them. Not like having them hidden under your burka at all!

The people just needed to get organized! He felt an unstoppable, primordial energy running through him when he did yard work in the nude. He was sure that other people would feel it, too. They would KNOW not only that they had to do something to stop the corporate plunderers from killing the earth, but also that they COULD do something. Something real and concrete and definitive that would make a difference and unambiguously stop the juggernaut of destruction

Charles Morgan smiled to himself as he contemplated the ramifications of his vision of nudity solving all of the world's problems of hunger, disease, and war. He found it funny and ironic that the only people who would oppose this solution from the point of view of a political class with vested (pardon the pun!) interests, would be the suicide bombers (since the idea of walking around in the nude with a suicide vest strapped to your chest was more than slightly ludicrous), the people who wanted to carry concealed weapons around, the people who wanted to sell explosives and concealed weapons, the people who wanted to sell you a closet full of next year's fashions when this year's still hadn't yet been worn, the purveyors of junk food, who endemically relied on the convention of clothing and in particular ill-tailored, loose-fitting clothing to cover up their crimes, the big pharma companies who wanted to sell billions of diet pills, etc.; in short, the worst sort of people in the world who made their "living" promoting war and dysfunction and disease, crime and poverty, and the false utopias of the corporate welfare state. Heck no, we don't want people to be able to walk around in the nude! That wouldn't be any good for our profits! Charles Morgan could see them squirming if and when the movement really gathered steam

But he had to go about things carefully. He couldn't proselytize the movement because people hated proselytizers. It was like committing an act of violence when you were in an argument with somebody. All future discussions then centered on the act of violence rather than on the issue being argued.

If you were accused of proselytizing, people would dismiss you as just another proselytizer instead of giving much thought to what you were saying. So rather than fervently telling people that they should garden in the nude, because it was good for them and good for the world, he would have to lead for the most part by example, and hope that enough people saw the sense in what he was doing to follow him. It was a tough path to follow that he was setting for himself in this quiet quest for self-realization. A tough row to hoe, as they say. But it was a sound one, too. For if nobody followed him, he could hardly be disappointed. He could hardly have been said to have wasted his time. And if people did follow him, as he hoped, it would be a complete bonus, "all gravy" as they say. Then his dream of self-realization and returning the world to the way it should be rather than allowing it to destroy itself would be fulfilled. And since he was mature enough to realize that not everyone was lucky enough to achieve actual 100% self-realization in life, or that everyone's dreams came true (despite the fact that many people's dreams did come true, especially for those people who lived in his hometown) he accepted this path for himself, this arc for the rest of his life, earnestly, completely, and resolutely, realizing that if he failed, at least he had dared a mighty thing, and had not been content to dwell in "the perpetual twilight which knows neither victory nor defeat".

He knew the path he was setting himself on was a dangerous one, going up against the powers that be and the neo-fascists who were fast turning the country into a dystopian police state where they kept tabs on everybody, even good, innocent naturists. His father had told him not to end up in jail like he had. Charles Morgan knew that by setting out on this path he might end up in jail. Or in some other kind of bad trouble. But he didn't care. Something had to be done. He was filled with a terrible resolve, like those suicide bombers. Only he didn't have an explosive vest. In fact, he didn't have a vest at all.

"Molly, I have to leave tomorrow. The country needs me." Then he proceeded to tell her what he had learned about the government's surveillance of innocent, peace-loving naturist communities.

12

The Movement Gathers Steam

It was during the last years of the Bad President's reign that the nude yard worker movement gathered critical mass. The economic policies of the Bad President and his henchmen, and the coteries of plutocratic advisors that they employed and that hung around them as members of his kitchen cabinet, were so skewed and hopelessly unfair that they finally, inevitably began to bear terrible, bitter fruit for the nation. Economic output slowed, GDP went down, factories shuttered up, people got laid off and lost their homes. The Bad President and his friends had conceived of the world as a dog-eat-dog world where only the strongest survived. And because they conceived of the world in this manner, that is what the world became. The scorched earth policy that they had pursued elsewhere in the world followed them home as the reputation of America got so bad around the world that nobody wanted to buy her products or own her currency anymore. An economic depression that made the Great Depression of 1929-1939 look good began to grip the nation as people lost confidence in the future and in the ability of their leaders to do anything about the situation. It was during such depressing socioeconomic circumstances that people discovered nude yardworking. To them, nude yard working was a dream come true, a blessing from heaven. Everyone had the potential to do it. Becoming nude was within reach of everybody. It was not an expensive thing that you had to buy and it did not require an extensive education. There was no special aptitude required, no difficult-to-obtain licenses, and no red tape. Nude yard working was something they could all grab hold of and understand because, well, they could all relate to their own nudity. And as far as gardening went, well you can imagine that people had to eat despite having no money so victory gardens sprouted up everywhere. Everybody had one. Some were large and more than an acre in size. And others were small, with just enough tomato plants, some cucumbers and broccoli to provide for their family. People on the edge and not so much on the edge discovered that they could forget about their money troubles, and garden in the nude, for fun and profit, and to survive, and there weren't enough cops to stop them all. If they did get arrested, once in a while, at least that meant they would get a few hot meals in the county jail, courtesy of the taxpayers who were probably a little better off than they were, and then be released.

Furthermore, it came to pass that for the most part, people left other people who were working in their yards and gardens alone if they were nude because they thought that they were a little bit crazy and not worth the trouble to bother. It wasn't as if gardening in the nude was an especially lewd or lascivious type of behavior anyway, which most state statutes required it to be in order for an arrest to be made under the public nudity laws. Oh no, nude gardeners were going about their business in a most determined, gritty, defiantly unsexual way. Generally their knees and hands got dirty, their hair got matted and sweaty, and if you got too near to them you might not like the way they smelled, and if they bent over they might pass wind in your face. But part of the point of it was to announce to the world that they wanted to be left alone. Gardening in the nude was like planting a giant "Don't Tread on Me!" flag on the front lawn, which most people understood and respected. And so like bio-diesel, car-pooling, flex-hours, telecommuters, and a resurgence in carbon-free bicycling, nude gardening gradually became an accepted fixture of the American landscape.

There is an old saying attributed to Lenin which is: "*There are decades where nothing happens; and there are weeks where decades happen.*" That summer in America the nude yardworker movement took off like one of Elon Musk's rocket's, well the kind that don't blow up anyway. Everybody everywhere all at once just started doing it. It is just the most extraordinary thing, that a movement can reach critical mass so fast, like the Occupy Movement did in the Fall of 2011 or the Black Lives Matter protests did in the Spring of 2020, or the MeToo movement in 2019. Or the naked yardworker movement did that Summer.

People who lost all their money in the stock market started to do it. Math teachers did it. Garage mechanics who spent all day with cogs and gears and grease up to their arms did it.

Veterinarians did it. (They began to relate to the animals they treated better afterwards.) All sorts of people who you wouldn't expect did it. Take Harvey Slentz, for example.

Harvey Slentz lived in the country and made his living as a plumber and sanitary inspector and to him, living in the country meant that you had to look down into your bottle of beer before you took a swig off of it to make sure a fly hadn't landed down in there and was floating belly up. That is if he set his beer down on the job and went back to it a half an hour or twenty minutes later, glad it was still kicking around, and glad that he had been fortunate enough to find it again (but somewhat sad that it was appreciably warmer than it used to be). And he did that a lot. Because what the hell, if you couldn't drink while sweating nasty copper joints that never seemed to want to fit together right, what could you do? I mean what damn rights did you have any-more in this country anyway, if you couldn't do that, thought Harvey. So Harvey did that alot, and Harvey also became a nude yardman because his rights were important to him and he wasn't the type to be happy just thinking about them, he wanted to exercise them, too, just like he wanted to drink beer on the job, not just think about. Truth be known, although Harvey drank on the job, whenever he could find his old beers and/or was rich enough to afford new ones, none of his joints leaked and all his plumbing worked fine. He was an excellent plumber. He was an excellent plumber because, besides discovering that his rights, if seldom exercised would soon be lost, Harvey had also figured out that plumbing was a thinking man's game, and that if you figured out what you had to do in your head before you started cutting and threading pipes, you would make your job a whole lot easier, and be much more successful at it. Many people criticize those who drink on the job. Its fashionable to do so in some quarters. But I've seen tugboat captains and art teachers and famous actresses drink on the job and I actually think they do a BETTER job as a result of it. It keeps their edge up. And let's not forget Winston Churchill who drank heavily all through World War Two. Did Hitler, the abstemious one, the vegetarian who didn't drink, win that war? Oh, no siree!

Harvey became a nude yardman by first going around his house in the nude, never setting foot out in the yard where people could see him. Hell, if I can't walk around my own house in the nude without feeling bad about it, what can I do, asked Harvey of himself one day. So he walked around his house like a parading king, feeling good about it, and wondering why he hadn't done it more often before. Then gradually he started going outside without his clothes on and then eventually began pruning his trees, raking the leaves and mowing the lawn without his clothes on 100% of the time. You see it took him some time to get his courage up, but eventually he did.

Then there was Leonard Martin from Coos Bay Oregon who loved fat girls. Leonard had lost his job who knows how many times and had worked in so many different industries that he didn't quite know what to put on the "Occupation" line when he filled out his IRS form 1040 in the years when he was lucky enough to have to fill one out. He met the nude yardman at noontime in the smoky, inky blackness of a small, mom and pop 24-hour casino in Dillon, Montana playing nickel slots when he was down to his last nickel. Charles Morgan had come in out of the natural daylight to get change for a twenty dollar bill so he could make a phone call...and *halleluiah!*...here was salvation. Leonard sidled over to him. Could he by chance borrow ten bucks? Of course, said Charles Morgan, who could see, despite the smoke and inky blackness, that the fellow was a good fellow, just down on his luck a bit, and besides he was pretty much always philanthropic and generous of spirit prone to giving the odd sawbuck to polite vagrants, even if they only had one tooth, smelled funny, or hadn't shaved in a while. The two of them had hit it off, gotten to talking, and then hitch-hiked to Helena together to see Leonard's cousin, the decision to go being made over a beer at a local tavern.

Leonard loved fat girls because they were low maintenance. They didn't need fussing over, but they liked to fuss over him. They cooed and caressed him as he lay in bed and smoked his cigarettes after making love. They were genuinely in love with him and he with them, in a way. Of course he didn't stay in love with any particular one of them for long because he was always moving on from one job to the next and having to leave one town for another without much actual notice to anybody. He carried all his belongings in a backpack so he could do that. As long as he had a small wad of cash in his pocket and a pack of cigarettes he was ready to hit the road at a moment's notice. If there was a hurricane in Florida that had caused widespread damage and a call went out for temporary emergency workers to help sift through the rubble, blam! He would hit the road in an hour or two after he heard the news on the television, even if his then current girlfriend was still at work and he couldn't say goodbye; heck, he could always call her when he got to where he was going, a thought which assuaged his guilt many times, but which intended action didn't always occur. He credited his extreme mobility as his most important personal asset. You see he was always afraid the job opportunities that he imagined existed in those remote localities would disappear if he didn't move quickly enough. And sure enough they would disappear if he didn't move fast enough. Like that cushy federal firefighting job in Wyoming had! So he had learned to adapt to the exigencies of his self-imposed lifestyle. *The early bird catches the worm,* he would say to himself as he stuck his thumb out and hitchhiked across this great country of ours from one job to another, the future, one great vista of opportunity in the direction of travel, and the past, where he was coming from, just a pleasant memory, and a fading one at that.

He dipped his toe into the waters of nude yardworking, so to speak, because it appealed to him in a basic sort of way. He didn't have many clothes in his backpack. He couldn't carry proper gardening apparel around with him and he couldn't afford to wash his clothes if he got them dirty kneeling in the dirt. *And* he was a minimalist by the necessity of his mode of living and existential temperament. So the fact that he could strip off his clothes and do yardwork in his birthday suit suited him just fine. He felt like a king doing it. Yes, he felt like effing Louis the XIV strolling around the Versailles orangery in his birthday suit; for surely he had read somewhere that Louis had liked to stroll around the grounds of that great palace without any clothes on. Hadn't he? Well, it sounded good anyway, even if he had just imagined it. Even if the good king Louis hadn't really done that, he might have, and probably should have, just to show everybody that he could do whatever he wanted.. That was the way kings were supposed to be. They had to do wild and crazy things every now and then to show everybody who was boss. Yes indeed! To show everybody that you were fit to govern you had to show every-one that you yourself were a bit *ungovernable.* You had to show them that you were cut from different cloth than the ordinary man. You had to show them that you marched to the beat of a different drummer. So Leonard liked the idea that by gardening in the nude it showed that he was cut from different cloth than the average man, and that he marched to the beat of a different drummer.

When Charles Morgan first taught Leonard how to do yard work in the nude, he had been hesitant and had resisted at first. He thought maybe it was a faggy thing to do. But then he had said "Oh, what the heck!" and took off all his clothes and helped pick apples at an orchard in Washington State where they were for the harvest, getting paid by the bushel. Leonard embraced the movement because he was a natural born rebel. He hated rich people and he hated The System. He purposely spent all his money whenever he got any until he was broke so he wouldn't have to be 'miserable' like most of the rich people he knew. (There *are* people like that out there.) In fact, when Charles Morgan left him he was teaching others how to enjoy gardening *au natural* and having a good time at it, believing that by doing so he was getting his own personal revenge on The System; for instance for that time the FEMA bureaucrats had *not* hired him to help pick up after that second Florida hurricane after he had hitchhiked all the way down from Oregon to help them. The bastards!

Or take Henry Reed. Henry Reed was an Eagle Scout who had all 121 Merit Badges. He started doing nude yardworking because he thought it was an All American thing to do, in keeping with the Constitutional right of self expression and the spirit of liberty. His conception of what was All American and what was not might have been slightly different than the average bear's. But certainly no better or worse. Anyway, it made him feel good. And when he got his girlfriend to do it with him, it made him feel even better.

And David Rockefeller, the famous rich banker? He began to do his yard work in the nude. David was an avid gardener, and a nonagenarian. He had lost his beloved wife many years ago, and doing his yard work in the nude helped him feel young and happy again, and reminded him of the times he and his wife used to walk around his Pocantico estate in the nude. Not too often, of course, because there were lots of people around the place back then when she was alive, but once in a while nonetheless, mostly under a full moon and quiet skies, among the formal gardens. Then they would.....ah, well, no need to remember that! Gardening in the nude added years to his life, and after he started doing so, his philanthropy increased tenfold.

And Henry Kissinger? Can you believe Henry Kissinger, that pompous old so-and-so with the fake German accent began to garden in the nude? Well, he did. He claimed he never felt so good.

The unspoken code of the nude yard worker movement was, well, simple bliss. That subtle, nebulous quality of existence that everybody yearns for but never quite seems to have. Bliss is something you have to achieve yourself. It isn't available in any store. There is no one to make an appointment with to obtain it. It can't be arranged for pickup or shipment through Amazon, or anywhere else on the internet. It is extremely rare and hard to find, this exquisite state of being. But doing yardwork in the nude brings it on. Why? Well because you are communing with Nature, which is sort of always a prerequisite for bliss. And you are doing something that is important for yourself, your species, and the whole world, really. You can withdraw into your own private bubble, your own world, your own backyard and do your own thing and nobody will bother you. Except the prudes, of course. But they don't matter. Remember that old saying. "Those who mind don't matter, and those who matter don't mind"? Well, that pearl of wisdom pertains in this situation. You are not being a common lunatic by doing it. You are being an uncommon one, Louis the 14th walking around his orangery, not King George the III talking to a bush. And your endorphins and oxytocin levels go through the roof!

So when was it, exactly, that almost everyone in the world started taking notice of the nude yardworker phenomenon which was sweeping the United States? When Home Depot started offering weekend classes in nude yardwork in order to boost the sales of garden tools and shrubs from their horticultural section? When the pundits on FOX News started changing their point of view from condemning nude yardwork as a sign of moral decay, to applauding it as a symbol of the dignity and supreme rights of the individual that David Rockefeller's grandfather, J.D. Rockefeller was always talking about, and had engraved on his memorial plaque in New York's Rockefeller Center Plaza? When CNBC ran a segment on the new business opportunities that went along with the new movement? (They were pretty slim for the apparel industry, of course, except for funky, custom kneepads and baseball caps and that sort of thing. But for suntan lotion, garden tools, and vegetable seeds? My god, demand for those things was soaring!)

When Indian television, Russian television, European television, and Chinese television correspondents who were covering the ever peculiar American popular scene themselves shed their clothes to partake in a little clothing optional tilling of select plots of suburban American soil for the benefit of their international viewers?

In human history, the pendulum swings back and forth between periods of State Control and Individual Power. During the building of the pyramids, State Control was ascendant, whereas during the American pioneer era, the power of the individual was. During the period that concerns us in our examination of the nude yardman's determined campaign to bring nude yardworking to the lawns and gardens of America, the pendulum had swung so far to the side of State Control, that it wasn't funny. In fact, it was down-right oppressive. That was the price of stability. Generation after generation of duly-elected politicians had been sent down to Washington to make good, and had passed law after sanctimonious law until there were so many laws on the books, that nobody even knew how many there were anymore. People like William Simon, the erstwhile Treasury Secretary, had written books like *A Time for the Truth* trying to tell the American people about the danger of too many laws, but it didn't seem to do any good. The process just rolled along inexorably. Like the self-made patriarch who pays his incompetent son-in-law to stay home rather than go to the office and make costly mistakes in the family business, it would have been better if the American people had simply paid politicians not to go to Washington sometime around 1954 or so, and simply lived with the laws they had on the books. But that did not happen. Anyway, since laws affect everyone, and since criminal law affects people more drastically than other kinds of law, a preternatural fascination with criminal law began to develop in the American psyche. Television shows like Law and Order, Special Victims Unit, and CSI: Miami, and COPS became hugely popular. In fact, fully 5/8's of all television programming eventually concerned itself with criminal law enforcement, a fact which could be discerned by a casual examination of the weekly television programming schedule. But if you analyzed these shows in detail, you could see that they all repeated the same pattern: they were all, to a greater or lesser extent, merely an examination, in Peyton Place fashion, of the travails and intrigues, triumphs and failures, prides and prejudices of one nest of 'Flying Monkeys' or another. The names changed, but the characters and situations remained the same. And although they still continued to watch them on the surface, unconsciously Americans had grown tired of this lopsided, unwholesome fascination with the goings-on of The Dark Side. Thus when Charles Morgan's nude yard worker movement came along, it offered such a welcome relief to that type of hackneyed diversion, that people wanted to jump onto the band wagon that he and it presented with open arms, and with an energy and genuine earnestness that they might not otherwise have had if things had been going really well in America up until this time.

Another thing that helped the movement grow was an increasing recognition of the dangers of Nature Deficit Disorder. The existence of Nature Deficit Disorder (NDD) as an actual medical condition began to be recognized shortly after the nude yardman started taking off his clothes. Nature Deficit Disorder could occur in both children and adults but it was first noticed in children by pediatricians. It was noticed by the authorities that the disease soon became epidemic in the developed world. The symptoms were obesity, allergies, depressed immune system response, boredom, and lethargy. The cause of the disease was simple: people, and perhaps most importantly young people, were spending more and more of their time inside watching television, playing video games and surfing the internet, and less and less time going outside to have fun. They were, believe it or not, becoming addicted to things which had been willfully designed to addict them for purely commercial purposes.[5] In contradistinction, certainly God never designed a tree with the idea of addicting someone to its beauty!

Taking away the person's video games and Internet access only exacerbated the condition of those addicted as then a kind of incurable melancholy set in. Mothers who had lost a son or daughter to NDD formed support groups where they could get together and talk about their experiences and share their grief and anger. They formed a nationwide organization called Mothers Against Nature Deficit Disorder (MANDD). They held bake sales to raise awareness. They petitioned the various levels of the government to get the word out about the dangers of nature deficit disorder and to do something about it. Students who had lost brothers and sisters to the disease, seeing their mothers campaign the way they did, formed their own organization, Students Against Nature Deficit Disorder, with the obvious acronym, SANDD. "Don't Make Fun of Nature Deficit Disorder, or *IT* Will Make Fun of *You!*" and "NDD Kills!" were two of their slogans. Their posters showed before and after pictures of their friends and relatives who had succumbed to NDD. Before: Sweet, charming kids who didn't have a weight problem, and were all nicely dressed and had smiles on their faces. Afterwards: Pale-faced, slovenly-dressed kids with scowls and frowns on their faces who looked like they didn't care about anything and were trying to get into the Guinness Book of Records on the basis of their weight and/or the amount of time they spent playing video games without sleeping, or going outside.

The people who were involved with MANDD and SANDD were very serious, earnest, goodhearted people, trying to do The Right Thing. When they gave their stamp of approval to the nude yard working movement as a promising method to combat the scourge of NDD, the movement got a real boost.

As the nude yardworker movement took off and gathered momentum, there were other splinter groups, copycat organizations, and 'wanna-be' movements that formed. There was the nude garbage collectors' movement, the nude traffic director's movement, the nude tractor driver's movement, the nude ballet dancer's movement (they didn't have far to go behaviour-wise because their normal attire did not consist of too many clothes on to start with!), the nude baseball pitcher's union, the nude meter maids union, and so on. These had varying degrees of success. Some lasted a decent amount of time, others fizzled out before too long because they didn't have the same legitimacy that the nude yardworker movement had. In most people's mind's 'yardwork' was associated with 'gardening', and 'gardening' with the 'Garden of Eden', where Adam and Eve were known to be cavorting around in their birthday suits as god had meant for them to be; whereas most people weren't too sure that god had actually intended for meter maids to be tooling around in their three wheelers without any clothes on. And so it went with other organizations as well. But what was surprising or perhaps not so surprising given the parlous state of world affairs at this time in human history, was the sheer number of different groups and people who decided that clothing optional was the way to go and the way to be in just the same way that tattooing and body piercing took off. Altricious nude behavior just took off beyond all reasonable expectation, defying the most normally accurate social scientists and pundits. Because let's face it, there is something safe and secure about working and playing with your clothes on. Whereas there is something that feels kind of risky when you do things without them. Especially for the first time. And what everyone fears the most is being made a fool of. People were naturally fearful that if they started doing their yardwork in the nude, people would make fun of them. So the fact that large numbers of people, some estimate the number was in the millions, were willing to throw caution to the wind and had the courage to experiment with this new form of self-expression cum self-realization which felt gimmicky, but actually was quite natural is quite remarkable

So, yes, splinter groups began to split off from the main nude yardworker movement who, encouraged by the success of that movement, claimed that it was good to do other things in the nude as well. We have mentioned some, but there were others. For instance, there was the nude kitchen worker's movement, the nude maids society, the nude policeman's athletic club, the nude tennis players association, the nude professional golf association, the nude parent teacher association (who had their meetings in the nude), the nude rotary league, which had their luncheon meetings in the nude, and the nude lion's club, which elected their presidents in the nude. Trapeze artists began to perform in the nude, as did lion tamers, and concert cello players. There were the nude loggers for jesus and the nude visiting nurses association. There was even a group of nude tailors who claimed that it was easier to take measurements and sew clothes together in the nude, and the results came out better, because while they were nude they could better imagine how the way the clothes they were making would fit on a nude human body. People who bought clothes from such tailors raved about them. They always fit perfectly and never chafed or felt tight in any spots.

There had always been nude, or semi-nude donut servers, cocktail waitresses, and lap dancers, but soon occupations started sprouting up that had not traditionally been associated with nudity in the past. For instance it was now possible to find a hair stylist who would style your hair in the nude or a manicurist or pedicurist who would give you a manicure or pedicure in the nude. Barbers, who displayed the traditional red white and blue revolving pole outside their shops, did not go in for this type of showy, *avant garde* behaviour, however. They were traditionalists, and conservative. They knew what it was like to wait all morning for a single schmoe to show up to get a twelve dollar haircut. They survived by toeing the line. Whereas, the hair stylists who had always been the more liberal types in their approach to hair styles and pricing, began to enthusiastically experiment with nude "dos".

The nude hairstylists' union, a union in the sense of an association of like-minded individuals and not in the sense of a tightly organized legal entity with bylaws and subscription agreements which represented labor interests, even tried to appear before one state legislature to lobby for official recognition as a separate license category, but they fell short of their goal.

Fortunately or unfortunately while these movements enjoyed sporadic success they never caught on as fully and completely as the nude yardworker movement did. First of all, in some occupations, clothes were actually an asset to the performance of the job, not a hindrance. Nude policemen without bullet-proof vests did not enjoy an intrinsic advantage over the policemen who did wear such protective clothing in hostage rescue situations involving large numbers of desperate murderers with lots of guns and ammunition holed up in an impregnable fortresses, for instance.

Furthermore, using this logic it is clear why a movement representing nude firefighters or bomb disposal experts never materialized to any significant degree.

Nude yardworking is something that can be done by the individual, and does not depend on group participation.

With every step taken while in the nude, you are more conscious of your body. The condition of your physique becomes more important to you. If you feel a certain heaviness or rotundness in your midsection or bottom, or imbalance in your gait, or upper body weakness with your clothes on, it is magnified a hundred times with your clothes off. Likewise, if you feel more upright and strong, and a sense of Kundalini rising with your clothes on, then with your clothes off, that too is magnified a hundred times. So that when you sit down to dinner the image of your misshapen body is sharper and more clear in your mind and less likely to be pushed aside and forgotten and the desire to improve it is more insistent. If you are a man, the fact that your belly sticks out more than your willy, making you a member of the infamous "Dickey-Do Club ("Your belly sticks out more than the dicky do!") becomes impossible to ignore. Thus walking around without any clothes on is not only a solution to the problem of obesity and lack of regular exercise, but it is also a self-reinforcing solution, meaning that the more you walk around in the nude the better your physique becomes and the better your physique becomes the more likely you are to walk around in the nude, since you feel better about showing off your body. (In other words, you are much less likely not to eat well and to forget to do your daily exercises when you are a nudist. The mental image you have of your body becomes paramount, and that's a good thing.)

You can go longer periods of time without eating anything as a full or part-time nudist, since you can look at the fat in your belly or thighs, which is unmistakable without any shirt or pants on, and say "Well, I guess I can live on that for awhile!" Portion control becomes easier to accomplish, the main event at meal-time instead of an afterthought. Fruits and vegetables figure more and more prominently in one's diet. Blood pressure levels decrease from high to normal, and cases of both Stage I and Stage II hypertension disappear almost as if a magic wand had been passed over individuals after they begin gardening in the nude.

Knowing that you can, all by yourself without anybody's permission, experience the pleasure of gardening in the nude is like having an all expenses paid, first class ticket to the vacation destination of your dreams in your pocket and knowing that you have it there all safe and ready to be used as you go about your daily business. And many people describe the experience of putting your clothes on once again after a thrilling episode of nude yardwork, and returning to the "normal" world is like having a holiday end or leaving a lover. It is always a bummer. At the worst, emotionally traumatizing. And at the best, bitter-sweet. But then of course, life does have its ups and downs.

In the art world, nude subject matter enjoyed a new, powerful resurgence. It was no longer taboo to paint the human form without any clothes on. It was no longer primarily just in paintings and sculptures from the past that people saw nude figures. Contemporary artists began to make up for their lack of including them before, except in odd, exceptional, spiteful ways, with a vengeance. Their compositions became filled with joyous, relaxed poses of nudes showing their classical beauty and grace in natural surroundings and doing chores around the house. Nude models became so much in demand that they were well nigh impossible to find, even though advertisements for them filled up the newspapers. The cost of hiring a nude model went from $25 an hour to $250 an hour in just under a year, and the ones you could get were impatient and sassy, or else not very pretty.

People went to the mall in the nude and shopped in the nude, forgetting that they had just been yardworking. At first most of them got arrested.

But then the nation's jails started overflowing with people who had been arrested for violation of public nudity ordinances. And the problem got so out of control that police, for the most part just stopped writing tickets for public nudity, and judges dismissed them on a summary basis. So it was that America, at least for the most part, became a clothing-optional place, a nation where clothes were as much forgotten when going out in public as remembered.

As a result of all the attention focused on doing things in the nude, people began to dream extensively about doing things in the nude that they had never dreamed of before. Psychiatrists began to experience unusually heavy volume of reports of people dreaming that they were doing strange, heretofore unheard of things in the nude: building bridges, and marching in the band playing saxophone[6]. What did it mean, for instance, if a 48 year old man, who had never skinny-dipped in his life suddenly had a dream about skinny dipping with all the members of his bible study class? They scratched their heads for answers, but they really didn't know. It wasn't like the earlier dreams of showing up in class without your underwear on which were much easier to psychoanalyze.

Because it was an interesting new phenomenon, articles about the nude yard worker movement began appearing with increasing frequency in newspapers and magazines. The Sunday Supplement for instance carried the story of how Charles Morgan taught Nuriel Bambini, the infamous Dr. Doomsday, a macro-economist at a famous New York university, how to do yardwork in his rooftop garden. Afterward he got in the habit, Nuriel felt so good about it that his macro-economic forecasts started to take on a decidedly optimistic tone. Wall Street couldn't figure out what was going on. They scratched their heads, puzzled by his change of tone. But his forecasts in the past had been accurate, so they listened to him and the stock market went up 20%!

Or take this conversation which occurred between Sam Sperry, the saxophonist, and Tamara Jones, the owner of a nightclub in Chicago where he played, which appeared in the lifestyles section of The Chicago Sun. According to the article, the two of them were looking at his brass alto saxophone, gleaming yellow in some places, but burnished brown with age in others.

"How much do you want for it Sam?," Tamara asked.

"Six hundred. If the Club buys it for six hundred, together with the seven hundred they owe me for the performance, I'll have thirteen hundred. Imagine the idea of starting out a fresh chapter in your life with $1,300! But that's what I'll have and that's what I want to do.

"But why do you want to do this, Sam? Clue me in! You're a gifted musician! What's the idea of quitting now? You make a lot of people happy with your music."

"I know, but I'm 60 years old and I've had great ideas along the road, but never had any time to do them. Ideas like Clarkson had in 1895 that gasoline is going to be the lifeblood of this country. I can't say where those ideas will take me, if anywhere. But I want a chance to explore them and develop them, and I can't do that playing music. You know what the life of a musician is like. You go from gig to gig with hardly any money in your pocket. You barely have enough to eat and pay your motel bill most of the time.

"But Sam. You're a gifted musician," Tamara pleaded

"Maybe, but I am going to retire to the country and do yard work in the nude. My brother has a place down in Mississippi and I'm going to do that for a while and contemplate green, growing things. But don't worry, my time in Chicago with you and your club will always occupy a special place in my heart."

Yep, that conversation really took place, at least according to the author of the article.

The nude yard worker movement spawned a revolution in advertising. Madison Avenue advertising agencies and mainstream advertisers, to the limits they were allowed to by law, began to advertise breakfast cereal, and soap cleanser, and antacids, and used cars using cleverly nude or almost nude actors and actresses. Some wore only barrel hoops around their obviously nude bodies as they walked around in their commercials. Others were viewed by the camera from different angles which hid their private parts, but exposed the rest of them. The nude yardworker movement was hot, and Madison Avenue knew it. Nude advertising increased sales of some products 150%!

13

The Bad President Throws a Hissy Fit

In the solarium of the official residence upstairs in the White House, the Bad President and his wife were watching tv when a segment came on the evening news about how the nude yard-working movement was taking off in California. He picked up the clicker and was about to change the channel when his wife said "No, don't, honey… I want to watch this." So he reluctantly put down the clicker and slowly turned a shade of beet red which indicated his annoyance at the situation. And tried to look at the cover of a magazine on the coffee table and not at the tv, because he hated any mention of this new "fad" which was sweeping the country, and even making its way into the national news and daily intelligence briefings.[7]

But out of the corner of his eye he kept watch on his wife's face and could tell from her eyes that she was really interested in learning about this new movement. He wondered how far her interest would grow. Would she want to experiment? Would one day he look out his window and see her in her birthday suit carrying a hose or water sprinkler in the Rose Garden, perhaps accompanied by a handful of female aides who were in their birthday suits, too? The thought horrified him. And as he dwelt on it and magnified it in his mind until it horrified him more and more, and suddenly, what was the tiniest most remote possibility of her actually doing that became an absolute certainty, one that he was resolutely determined to prevent at all costs. It was probably then at that moment that he became determined to nip the nude yardworker movement in the bud and utterly destroy it and the man behind it, the utterly and completely harmless Charles Morgan, as unlikely a protagonist as ever there was one.

The next night it happened again. The Bad President and his wife were watching the evening news in the White House solarium again. A piece on the BBC America evening news broadcast came on about a local man who started doing his yardwork in the nude and how he was part of a growing nation-wide movement started by Charles Morgan Prendergast. The Bad President reached for the clicker which was on the coffee table with all fancy magazines on it. He didn't want to listen to that! His blood pressure skyrocketed everytime he heard about the Nude Yardman on the radio or tv.

"No, don't honey," his wife said. "I want to watch that!"

The Bad President didn't say anything. But he seethed inside. That damn Nude Yardman again! He reached for a pretzel. He swallowed it hard, discombobulated by what he had just seen on tv and it went down wrong. He started gagging.

"You aren't choking on a pretzel again, are you dear?" his wife asked, still looking at the tv, but hearing her husband choking.

Just then the stuck pretzel got unstuck and he cleared his throat, reaching for a glass of water. "No, no. I'm fine," he managed to say. But the next morning he called an emergency meeting of his national security staff in the Oval Office. He didn't like the idea that his wife was more interested in finding out about the nude yardworking movement than she was in the fact that he was choking on his food. He was going to nip this one in the bud! Oh, yes-siree!

"I want him arrested!" the Bad President yelled as if in a fit. There was a pause. Then silence among those who had already gathered in the Oval Office for the meeting. No one knew if these angry yelling spells and fulminations of the Bad President were in fact symptoms of some as yet undiagnosed mental illness. They were all afraid to suggest that he find out. That would mean a complete medical examination and stopping him from seeing that quack doctor of his who gave him those mystery hypodermic injections when he asked for them. The mere suggestion might get one fired. Besides, the idea that the President of the United States was an absolute foil-hatted nutjob were negligibly small. He had after all been elected (ahem...eer!..ahhh...) by a majority of the people.

The Attorney General, who had been politically appointed, looked at the Bad President. And then looked down at his shoes without answering. Didn't his boss know that this was a nation of laws, that you couldn't just arrest somebody because you wanted to? "But Mr. President....in order for federal authorities to arrest someone they have to have done something wrong. In other words, they have to have broken some law. And it has to be a pretty serious breach you know because, well, we can't spend millions of dollars arresting every tom dick and harry who writes his telephone number on a dollar bill. As far as I can tell, he hasn't done anything wrong, federally, that is, that would give us cause to arrest him."

"Oh hell we arrest people for less every day. Where have you been, Stan? But I can see you're out of your depth. This ain't your bailiwick, is it? Get me my national security advisor. And my legal advisor, John Yoodleeyheehoo. They'll know what to do," he said with a wave of his hand. And then he looked out the window on a bright summer day, grimacing a little (perhaps suffering a little from All That Weight that was on his shoulders when he was making decisions which were for The Good of the Nation).

They had a hard time finding his national security advisor. He wasn't at his desk. Of course it is a well known fact that no one can ever find federal employees at their desks. But employees of *this* administration were supposed to carry beepers around which would allow their *jefe* to find them in a hurry. The theory was that electronic signals scrambled by a multi-million dollar device on the President's secretary's desk would shoot the desired beeper number over a secure line to the Pentagon where a special router would re-transmit that signal in a packet burst which contained about 40 gigabytes of extraneous information designed to fool people who might be listening to a receiver in a super secret military satellite control center buried deep in

Cheyenne Mountain, Wyoming. The signals would then be retransmitted to a sophisticated, $4 billion special-purpose military communications satellite network in geosynchronous orbit over the United States which would rebroadcast the message that the President sent to close members of the kitchen cabinet, the actual cabinet, staff members, etc. who might be anywhere, say across the corridor or in the same room, for instance. But in this case the National Security Advisor, that staunch stalwart man who always wore dark blue suits and never spoke unless he was spoken to, had turned his beeper off while he went with an old copy of Playboy to the bathroom to do his morning "bidness". So he didn't get the message from the top secret white house communications agency messaging system. But eventually one of the brighter than normal White House interns did find him over in the Old Executive Office Building in the most remote bathroom the building possessed.

"Ah, sir", said the intern to the national security advisor whose face he couldn't see, but whose shoes and dropped-down pants were visible beneath the open portion of the bathroom stall door.

"Yes, what is it confound it! Can't you see I'm doing my bidness?" Everybody in official Washington called it that. And had been doing so for generations.

"Ah, the President wants to see you asap in the Oval Office, sir."

"Ok. Tell him I'll be right there." A pause. "Who is that, anyway?"

"Carlton, sir. White House intern."

"Well Carlton, you found me this time. But the next time the president or anybody else wants me, you are going to forget to look in this bathroom." A pause. "Is that understood?"

"Yes sir."

The white house intern left, listening to the sound of toilet paper being unwound from the dispenser roll.

A few moments later the Bad President's legal advisor walked in to the oval office.

John Yodeleheewhoo wasn't the President's personal lawyer. That distinction fell to Thelma Brezinski-Kulpinsky. She and the President went back a long way. She had quietly greying hair and a mind like steel trap. Normally she could be relied on to issue a competent legal opinion. But her bid to become a Supreme Court justice had evaporated one day when it was discovered during the background investigation attendant to her nomination that 27 years ago she had hired an illegal immigrant to be her maid one summer. Her nomination was withdrawn and ever since then she had fallen into a sullen mood of self-pity that was impossible to shake her out of. If you gave her a job to do, she just wouldn't do it. Period. So even though she did continue to occupy a fashionable office in the West Wing, and came to work every day, the President didn't see her much anymore, except when she came up to the residence to cry on his shoulder when he did his best to cheer her up by recalling their early days together in Texas when they had lied their asses off in innumerable Court cases and gotten away with it.

John Yodeleheewhoo's name wasn't really John Yodeleheewhoo. His real name was John Y. Hu. But everybody called him John Yodeleheewho because of the singsong way in which he rendered his opinions. The Bad President's was, after all, an administration where nicknames were encouraged. John Y. Hu, the Presidents legal advisor, was of Chinese extraction and had been taught English by a Swiss missionary school in China. When one went into his office they usually found him standing by the window fussing over one of his orchids or "orchid projects" as he liked to call them, because sometimes an actual orchid-like flower on the plant he was tending was somewhat hard to find, or by the wall adjusting the precise frame angle of one of the many pictures that hung there.

Some people wondered why they never found John Yodeleheewhoo at his desk reading a legal brief, perhaps with his feet up. But they never did. The President wasn't bothered by that, however. He said John Yodeleheewhoo 's understanding of the law was "innate". That he didn't need to read the law because it was all "in his head". That the fellow was a legal eagle was obvious. Who else could determine in the twinkling of an eye that most things the President said were "spot on", legally? Who else could determine in the twinkling of an eye that the President didn't have to follow the bothersome laws that Congress was writing for him just because the Constitution said so? If Lincoln could suspend *habeas corpus,* and FDR could withhold knowledge of an impending attack on Pearl Harbor, then the Bad President could do what he wanted to, too. And John Yodleleeheehoo made sure he could, legally and properly, or at least with the semblance of legality, with presidential "signing statements" that he came up with whenever the Bad President signed a new piece of legislation into existence, wonderful pieces of pro executive power propaganda which said that although the bill said one thing, it could really mean quite another. What a clever fellow!

Because of the delay in finding him, John Yodeleheewhoo was already sitting in a chair in the Oval Office when the national security advisor walked in. The national security advisor had left the cherished 14 year old copy of Playboy he was reading in a carefully locked safe in his office where he kept the Single Integrated Operational Plan (SIOP), the budgets of so-called "black programs" and other important stuff he didn't want people to see because he knew how much his boss hated pictures of nude women and things having to do with nudity. Only he had the combination to that safe and there was a self-destruct mechanism in place that would destroy its contents if anybody else tried to break in so there wasn't much chance of anybody finding it there who wasn't supposed to. The fact that somebody else might need to access the Single Integrated Operational Plan ("The Big Bad Nuclear War Plan") or one of the other Top Secret documents in an emergency hadn't escaped him, but if Hilary could get away with storing thousands of classified documents on her home server, then hell, he could get away with "forgetting" to give someone else the combo to his office safe.

The Bad President was at his desk reading a memo somebody had sent him about what seemed like an epidemic of unexplained animal mutilations in the country and looked up when the National Security Advisor walked in. He gladly dropped the bothersome memo down and rose from his chair to greet him. "Hello Jason. Catch you at a bad time, did we?" There was a slight smile on the President's face for the reason that he had been informed that his national security advisor had been summoned from the bathroom in the Old Executive Office Building where he had been performing his morning "bid-ness" (See, everybody in Washington uses that expression!)

The President then walked over, dropped in a chair, and addressed everyone that had assembled in a morning fireside chat kind of way. "Good morning gentlemen. I've invited you here because......" he squirmed a little bit in his chair. "Well, we have a *situation*.... and its not a real *situation* you understand like we had with the bomber pilot who took the *nukular* joy ride, where we had to go down to the Situation Room and discuss it and all, but it's a *situation* nonetheless, OK?" He winked at both of the men conspicuously. "And I don't want anybody to know we have *this* situation, if you understand. This is strictly on the QT."

The President looked at his national security advisor who was busily scribbling notes on a yellow legal pad. "Jason, what's that you're doing? Taking notes again? How many times have I told you this administration is a "No Notes" administration. This stuff is supposed to be committed to *memory*." The President tapped his right forefinger against his temporal lobe three times for emphasis of the point. The National Security Advisor sighed wistfully, looked straight ahead, and put his pen away.

"Where was I? Oh yeah. Right! This Nude Yardman fellow is going around the country ruining the morals of the land. Now you guys know I'm against it. And it ain't because I've got a small weiner and want everybody to wear clothes!" he snorted. Not seeing the effect he was looking for he continued on. "I want an excuse to shut this guy down, permanently. Which means forever. And it has to be a good *legal* reason, that will stand up in court." He paused and then turned to his Legal Advisor.

"John, I know you have an opinion on this. Let's have it."

The legal advisor who had been given a fashionable west wing office instead of his normal office down in the Justice Department building to be more on hand when the actual making of policy was done, giggled a little nervously, and then yodeled three different notes all at once in quick succession with his warbling voice and said, "I'm with you on this one. It disgusts me too. But my concern here is that what this fellow is doing, as despicable as we may find it, to a federal Court would be considered merely as an expression of his First Amendments rights."

"Well that's what I brought you here to tell us about," the Bad President said congenially. "How can it be legal and considered part of a person's First Amendment rights to dance naked in a strip club or to serve donuts topless in Florida, but not considered Freedom of Speech if you're out there gardening in your birthday suit. Or more precisely", the Bad President's eyes narrowed darkly as he spoke this last phrase. "To teach people how to garden in their birthday suits!"

"Well, perhaps we could find a reason to arrest him for a violation of the 1918 Alien and Sedition Act.... has he ever made a statement denouncing the United States?"

"No, not that I'm aware of," said the Chief of Staff who had just popped in through the door. After he spoke he looked up to see if the plaster damage had been cured from the incident with the President's daughter and his six–shooter. He didn't want to be standing under it directly and have a piece fall down on him. Just to make sure he moved a bit to his side. Then he noticed a small spray of white powder on his left shoulder. He looked up again. The President and his two advisors were watching him.

"What are you doing Wendell?" The Bad pResident asked somewhat congenially.

"Just trying to get away from the ahh!..." He tried to point surreptitiously to the president at the ceiling. "The ah, you know," he said good-naturedly. "Those indoor rain clouds that are known to blow up suddenly in the Oval Office!" He said smiling. They all stared at him for a moment. They all knew he was a little kooky sometimes in a kind of good-natured and harmless way. Furthermore, everybody in the administration had heard about the incident with the president's daughter and the six shooter, even though it was considered bad form to talk about it since they weren't supposed to know about it, and talking about things that you weren't supposed to know about in Washington was tantamount to, well, political suicide. But the Chief of Staff could be excused. He had after all installed that marvelous electric shoeshine wheel in the outer hallway which had boosted everybody's morale. So he certainly wasn't all bad. Oh no-siree!

They got back to their intended conversation.

"Well then I think it would be very difficult to find him guilty of a violation under that Act," said John Y. Hu reflectively.

The President wasn't happy with the way this meeting and conversation was going. His finely tuned political acumen, his highly praised ability to read men and situations, his sensitive political antennae told him it was going nowhere fast. "Oh don't worry about that!" he said affably disguising his disappointment that they could not support his desire to jail the nude yardworker immediately and destroy the growing movement right off the bat. "You go back to your office and come up with a reason. I'm sure one will occur to you." He had after all relied on John Yodelheyheehoo, as an academic legal expert on "The Unitary Executive and Torture" memo to say it was okay to deny his prisoners their rights under the Geneva Convention and to find a way to destroy 92 different video tapes of torture after Congress had mandated that all the torture videotapes be preserved as evidence for an abuse of powers investigation.

"And what I want to know is, if we catch him, can we hold him without bail?" The Bad President asked precociously, getting ahead of himself somewhat and ahead of the thinking of the others in the room a little. "He's getting these crazy ideas of his from somewhere, and we need to find out where he's getting them from. And we need to find out what kind of organization he's got. Who his lieutenants are that carry out his orders? Who his admirers and supporters are? Find ways to disrupt his organization." He started rubbing his hands malevolently, as if he was washing them of sin.

"Mr. President... I'm not sure that he *has* an organization," the Chief of Staff said.

"You mean we won't get a chance to hold him without bail?"The Bad pResident said, clearly disappointed. He turned his gaze to his staunch National Security Advisor for help.

"Mr. President, don't look at me! I'm an expert on limited nuclear wars being waged by rump elements of the former Soviet Union gone rogue, the number of new carrier-killer missiles the Chinese built last year, the number of missing briefcase nukes in Georgia, or disabling launch codes on bombers gone missing on nuclear joy rides." His heavy brows knit together as he tried to remind the Bad pResident of the recent episode of the gay pilot who was protesting "Don't Ask, Don't Tell!". "What do I know about gardening? Or nudity? Once we had one guy at SAC who had his finger on The Button come into the office buck-assed naked passing out flowers. He had lost his nerve. We got rid of him. He's still in the Funny Farm, I think" said the National Security Advisor, referring to the military's off-limits psychiatric facility in Colorado where looney ex-Generals and ex-spies with thousands of deep, dark secrets were watched over by young zealous Christian evangelists from Colorado Springs who wore clean white uniforms and talked about the Lord with their slightly deranged medicated almost universally wheelchair bound and wrapped in bandages charges, when they weren't busy buggering each other (and denying it). "Until that starts happening more than just once or twice and we can trace those occurrences to Charles Morgan Prendergast, *and* we consider the further likelihood of it happening again to be a national security threat, I'm afraid I can't go along with you JB. We can't touch the guy. And if we bring trumped up charges against him, they'll fail. And waterboarding? Forget about it. Sorry, JB. You can't win them all. He got up from his chair. The meeting was over, as far as he was concerned. "Is this meeting over?" he asked politely for the sake of decorum. But he really wanted to storm out of there because he was a little pissed about having to interrupt his morning routine for such an asinine, inconsequential reason.

The Bad President took his cue. "More or less. So we'll just sit tight and wait for him to make a mistake?"

"That would be my advice JB," said the National Security Advisor.

"Mine too," said John Yodeleyheehoo. "Sorry, JB," he added.

"OK. I can live with that," said the Bad President. "I'll eat humble pie for awhile. And hope that no good nude yardman screws up somehow." His aides left the office.

"Get me "Haggar The Horrible" and the "Duke of Hazard" yelled the President to his Secretary through the open door after they left. This was, after all, as we have noted, an administration where the use of nicknames was encouraged. "Haggar the Horrible" was the Vice President, Dick Ruefricker, nicknamed thus because he always seemed to be carrying a heavy club with him wherever he went, physiognomically speaking. The "Duke of Hazzard" was Tony Hazzardly, an evangelical minister who ran one of the biggest "megachurches" in Texas and was the President's religious advisor. The Bad President wanted to consult with each of them about this nude yardman fellow and talk about what they should do about him. He didn't think either one of them would approve of such blatant nudity either. In fact, he was sure they would agree with him that something had to be done to stop what had the portents of being a very important menace to their shared values, and what was, in his opinion, a clear and present danger to the Nation.

14

Meanwhile, Back on the Home Front...

Meanwhile, back on the home front, during the time Charles Morgan had been away, Mary had gotten a job as a teller in a bank. It had done wonders for her. All these young, gorgeous guys would come in and flirt with her and she would feel thrilled and elated and filled with a hopeful sense of expectation about a possible relationship, perhaps one that would fill the void in her life that had been made when Charles Morgan left; and then she would see on the computer screen that the poor fellow only had a modest amount in his account. Hardly enough to elope on! Then her hopes would crash to the ground as if they had been a balloon pricked by a needle, and she would say to herself, "Another one bites the dust," even though she liked the guy well enough. And so Mary kept busy at the bank, making sure that all her accounts were properly balanced, and kept the way they were supposed to be. But she had not really met anybody yet that competed in her heart with the feelings she had for Charles Morgan. That no good Charles Morgan who had left her! Boy was she mad at him! She continued to garden in the nude every once in a while and that made her feel better every time she did it because it was like enjoying a gift that Charles Morgan had left her, and being so reminded of him, her thoughts would wing upward and she would forgive him and imagine that it might not be too long before he would be back, and that perhaps she should get herself ready for the time when he would arrive, and not encumber herself anymore with thoughts of those earnest fops and suitors who were vying for her attention. They were so very ordinary compared to Charles Morgan! A love like his could sustain a girl for a lifetime! But still, despite all that, she was pretty lonely, as you might expect. She was after all, a young, pretty girl and she didn't want to die a barren old spinster! Oh, no siree!

Uncle Winkle was slowly getting over the death of his best friend and playmate, the Oracle. One day Uncle Winkle was cleaning up. He noticed that the wicker basket of old receipts he kept on his bookshelf was getting to the point of overflowing, and it was his custom, at the end of every year, round about that time, to put them in a grocery bag, staple it up, and write the year on the bag with a black magic marker to preserve them for his accountant, when he finally got an accountant, that is. Someday. Hopefully. If he was lucky enough. OK, well maybe he would never get an accountant, but at least he was hoping that one day he would!

So he picked up a grocery bag from the pile of carefully folded paper bags that he kept, and emptied the basket of receipts into it. The only thing was, three nights ago, he had bought a lottery ticket which he had not checked which was among the receipts. It had came up a winner in the drawing, to more than $300 million the night before. So the winning lottery ticket to the Giga-millions(TM) drawing was laying there half buried under some of the other receipts that had been tossed in the basket willy-nilly and forgotten. It too was tossed into the bag and stapled shut. Shut into a world with all the other little pieces of paper that looked almost exactly like it, effectively and rather irrevocably camouflaged and cloistered away against further discovery for who knows how long, perhaps forever, but certainly beyond its valid redemption date.

And with it's sealing away, an alternate future was swept from Uncle Winkle's grasp. An alternate future of wealth and ease and comfort, filled with beautiful babes, sunny beaches, fast cars and luxurious homes, fine wines and well-tailored clothes. All the things that money can buy. Everything that Uncle Winkle had ever dreamed of, in fact, including the emancipation of numerous lobsters. All because he had forgotten to check his lottery ticket's numbers, so certain was he that he was not going to win. That was how far his negativity extended, to buying a lottery ticket and then, disgusted by his frivolous behavior, disgusted by the thought of subsidizing all the waste, fraud, and abuse of the state symbolized by the lottery, and all the false hopes and expectations of the unwashed masses who played it on a regular basis, refusing to check it to see if it had won. Uggh! Uncle Winkle did not understand that in order to be a winner, you have to think like a winner. And a winner does not think his numbers are going to be lose. Oh no siree! He thinks that they are going to win!

Later that day, completely oblivious to the alternate future that he had thrown away, Uncle Winkle was feeling particularly energetic and handsome so he decided to go to the *Shop and Go!* to see if he could bump into any of those young beauties who were by chance doing their grocery shopping that afternoon. A character in a novel he had read had bumped into his bride at the supermarket while they were both doing their shopping, so Uncle Winkle knew, and was hip to the fact, that things like that could happen in real life, for if he read it in a novel, he knew it could happen in real life. That was the way he thought about things anyway. So he brushed his hair and put on his best jacket and went down to the *Shop and Go!* But on the way, he faced a dilemma. Should he stop at the mailbox and get his mail? Or should he just go straight to the *Shop and Go?*

He didn't know what course of action to follow, and became worried that he didn't know. He was worried about stopping to get his mail, even though he hadn't collected it for two days, because of what he might find in the box. He knew that it COULD BE ANYTHING!!! (Anxiety attack!) Who knew who might have sent him a letter???!!!... The Patent Office telling him that a payment was due? The IRS telling him that the refund he was expecting had been miscalculated? A sneaky collection agency trying to get money out of him that he didn't really owe? An old flame, trying to see him again to rekindle their affair for some nefarious purpose? Perhaps that traffic court judge he had sent that letter to five years ago pointing out how flawed a ruling he had made was who had finally snapped, and was writing him to tell him that he was on his way to kill him? Heck, it could be anyone! The surprise and shock of getting the wrong kind of letter might totally destroy his rare, happy-go-lucky attitude, the one he had found himself in that afternoon, and put him in a bad mood. It was thus a risk to his plan of going down to the *Shop and Go!* and bumping into a beautiful woman to stop at the mailbox and pick up his mail. On the other hand, wasn't he being overly cautious, and a bit of a coward? He stopped to think about it, driving up to the mailbox and stopping beside it, but not opening it.

No, perhaps he wasn't, he thought. For after all, he had had some pretty bad news come in the mail before. It was best to be cautious. There was that old saying, "No mail is good mail." And there was a reason for it. Bad things did come in the mail. For every check you got, there were three bills. The mail was a known mood risk factor, an unnecessary random element in his plan of going down to the *Shop and Go!* and bumping into that rare sweety who would instantly fall in love with him and want to jump in the sack with him after they had carried the groceries back to his place, brushing aside all his self-doubts and worries about being eccentric, and not-so-terribly-rich.

Jeez, life was so terribly complicated. He couldn't even get his mail without thinking of all the bad things that could possibly happen to him. In the end, he did what every other normal person in the same situation would do: he steeled his mind to the possibility of finding *The Worst Possible Piece of Mail in the World* inside his mailbox... perhaps a piece of mail from his bank stating that his account was the victim of an identity theft attack, and had been drained of every last penny the day before yesterday by a man claiming to be him, and looking like him exactly, in all respects, except perhaps in retrospect for that one mole on his neck... or perhaps a letter from a medical testing laboratory telling him that he had a rare, incurable form of cancer and was probably going to die in three months...opened the mailbox... and found..... nothing! The box was empty.

Uncle Winkle breathed a huge sigh of relief. That bode well for his plan, didn't it? Not that Uncle Winkle was superstitious, for how could he be, being a scientist and all. But, well, let's just say he believed in luck, and in the ontological recapitulation of that luck. Yes, that was how it was. The ontological recapitulation of luck. And now with that piece of potentially bad luck out of the way, which would not now be recapitulated, it was going to be nothing but smooth sailing as he drove down to the *Shop and Go!* and had that rare, chance meeting with that one beautiful lass who, unbeknownst to herself, was already looking for him as a soul mate, that beautiful lass who was the lady of his dreams, to whom he could be a knight in shining armour as they discussed in scintillating terms over a bowl of cereal in the morning, the latest world news. Or the best kind of tomatoes to buy that time of year. It didn't matter what, really. Just as long as they were having that friendly, intimate conversation. He shut the mailbox, and drove off, feeling like a suddenly victorious Viking conqueror who had landed on the beach of a land he had chosen to invade without encountering any foes ready to put up a fight.

The next morning while Uncle Winkle was lying in bed trying to remember his dreams, for he was always very intrigued by them and put great store in their import, he let his unconscious mind run free, but he also had a glimmer of his conscious mind functioning, and it was during this time that he invented a new word, *astronomicality*. "Astronomicality", he heard his unconsciousness mind say to his conscious mind, "The property of being of or like astronomy." He was gladdened by the fact that his unconscious mind had provided a new, proper, dictionary-like word to his conscious mind. And it was such a great word! Uncle Winkle being an autodidact and scientist, of course loved astronomy, and he thought that he would probably like things that had the quality of being like astronomy, too. For three days he went around remembering that he had invented a new word, a special unique word that probably nobody else had ever bothered to think of before, and whenever he remembered it, it made him feel good inside. "Oh, yeah, '*astronomicality*', he would suddenly remember going about his everyday business, and then he would interrupt his mundane thoughts for a moment or two and just take delight at the new word he had created.

Now, the truth be known, Uncle Winkle had invented this word a night or two after watching a particularly exciting *Jeopardy!* episode wherein one of the categories was 23 Letter Words. 'Astronomicality' did not have 23 letters in it. It only had 15. But it was a big, long word like some of the other words that Alex Trebek had pronounced so effortlessly, each syllable of those sesquipedalian, poly-syllabic words rolling off his tongue like honey. And so it was probably a result of watching those pronunciations that his unconscious mind had brought together his love for astronomy and his love of new words in such a new and unique way. That is what he hypothesized, anyway.

He always marveled at the powers of the unconscious mind to invent new things and solve problems, without, it seemed, any effort at all, as if it was violating the second law of thermodynamics. But whenever Uncle Winkle dared to contemplate that this or that process might be violating the second law of thermodynamics, a law he cherished but which he supposed might be violated sometimes nonetheless, he was always careful to put a caveat in there, i.e., maybe it only *seemed* like the second law was being violated, whereas in reality maybe it really wasn't. That was the way his conscious mind worked. It was always very respectful of traditions and the establishment view but always ready to believe that perhaps the establishment view was sometimes wrong. It was a viewpoint that had served him well in life, and he congratulated himself for having developed it. In fact he had developed it to the point of it being pure dogma for him, and he was always very careful never to go too far out on a limb for some new theory or other, instead preferring to sit on the fence for however long it took for the truth to eventually come out.

Later that morning. Uncle Winkle was at the nursing home visiting his mother.

"It seems like the little Wiggle Worm has started a movement, Mother," he said.

"A what?" The nude yardman's grandmother seemed puzzled.

"A movement. You know, a large, growing number of like-minded people who like to do the same things, in this case yard work in the nude."

"Where did you read that?"

"In the *People* magazine down at the supermarket, in the magazine section. I read the copy standing there so I wouldn't have to buy it," said Uncle Winkle, thinking she would be impressed by his thriftiness.

"Oh, you're one of those people," said the nude yardman's grandmother, who was also Uncle Winkle's mother, with a disapproving tone in her voice.

Oh dear, thought Uncle Winkle. If she thinks that way about him for that, he certainly couldn't tell her anything about watching the lobsters in the *Shop and Go!* for then he would really be in hot soup.

"Well, we always thought he would grow up to be a nude yardman, didn't we?" She sipped her chamomile tea seemingly unmoved by the news. "Poor boy's had a tough life, what with his father being arrested and his mother going off to who knows where. Last time I heard from Charles was a postcard from Williamstown, Massachusetts. It's on my dresser there. He was helping the garden club decorate one of the town parks. He seemed to be doing all right."

"The article I read seemed to indicate he was doing just fine. And someone told me they'd seen him on *60 Minutes* recently. He's getting to be famous," said Bartholomew.

"Well, good for him," she said. Then she went back to reading her AARP bulletin trying to figure out whether the new changes to Social Security were going to affect her or not.

15

The Bad President Meets with Haggar the Horrible and Plots the Nude Yardman's Destruction

Two days after being called, the Vice President returned from his 'undisclosed location' which everybody knew (wink wink) was the Greenbrier Hotel in White Sulphur Springs, West Virginia where there was a gigantic underground bunker for government officials to ride out a nuclear war which had fallen into disuse. But the above ground amenities more than compensated for the peeling paint, leaking walls and dank smells underground. The golf course was especially luxurious, as were the many restaurants and shops in the elegant resort complex which had been around in one form or another since before the civil war.

He returned to go to the meeting with the Bad President that he had been summoned to over the phone.

"Did you bring your club?" the Bad President asked, looking up from the Resolute desk in the Oval Office where he was looking at pictures some relatives had sent him from the ski slopes in Aspen.

"Ha ha!" said Haggar the Horrible, whose real name was Ben Ruefricker and who was actually the Vice President of the United States. He didn't really carry around a club. That was just a left-handed joke that the Bad President occasionally played on him. What he did carry around was his heart, in a small black box. Actually it was a heart *pump*, technically called a LVAD, or a Left Ventricular Assist Device, and it was connected to his torso by two teflon coated tubes that carried his artificially flowing blood back and forth to his vascular system. He had had several heart attacks and was waiting for a heart transplant, but in the meantime the LVAD was performing the trick of keeping him alive.

"How was the Greenbrier?"

"Good except for the fact that those naked golfers were monopolizing the golf course again. Didn't get a single game in. We need to dig a big pit and push 'em all in with a bulldozer. Or build a big oven for them. Or maybe salt the clothes they leave in the locker room with bubonic plague fleas, or bedbugs or something."

He wasn't called Haggar the Horrible for nothing! He was slightly to the right of Attila the Hun. He had accidentally shot one of his friends in the face with birdshot on a recent hunting expedition and everybody remarked that he didn't seem particularly remorseful about it. He hadn't even gone to the hospital to visit the poor guy. "Oh, he's doing fine," he would say when somebody asked him about it.

"Well, that's what we need to talk about. That confounded nude yardman has thrown a monkey wrench into the well-oiled gears of this country, sapping the sinews of our national strength. Half the country is experimenting with doing yardwork in the nude and the other half is experimenting with doing other things in the nude. This needs to be stopped."

"Well of course!" said the Vice President, finally realizing what this conversation was going to be about. The President had been most secretive about it on the phone and he didn't quite know what to expect when he stepped into the room.

"The lawyers can't figure out what to do, so I wanted to hear from you," said the President with a dark undertone, squarely placing the ball in the Vice President's court and implying that he was counting on him to come up with a solution. After all the government was paying him a hefty salary, and the taxpayers expected him to do something for that money, not just go to Texas on birdhunts, or lollygag around a West Virginia golf course all day long.

"Here's what we have to do," Ben Ruefricker said, lowering his voice.

16

The Nude Yardman in Upstate New York

When the Bad President and his Vice President were plotting his destruction, the Nude Yardman was in Upstate New York.

What happened frequently in this part of the country is that old family farms which had been productive a hundred years ago, fell into disuse and disrepair. The families that ran them couldn't pay their taxes or couldn't make the mortgage payments, and they were sold at auction to disreputable and unscrupulous people who just wanted to make a buck off them, and didn't give a damn how they did it. Put a dollar into the proper upkeep of the lands while they lay fallow? Ha! That was a laugh! So the fields suffered, by lack of regular crop planting, with weeds, and shrubs, and saplings growing up in them in ceaseless profusion giving them an untended, jungle-like appearance. And the old family orchards, in particular, suffered, as without proper pruning, the apple and pear trees would start to sport large proportions of dead branches which would siphon off the water that should have been going to the live branches and nourishing the growing fruit. They were recognizable by almost all of the trees in the orchard having gnarly twisted branches jutting off into the air like the frozen forms of transmogrifying creatures escaping from the underworld, plastered with tumors and mold. And every year the situation on these abandoned farms would get worse and worse with nobody having the interest to do anything about them. There were thousands of old family farms like that, the land lying unproductive and fallow, and it was sad and ironic to consider that people down in the Amazon were burning down hundreds of thousands of hectares of rainforest to clear the land for farming when there was so much land already cleared and available in the United States that wasn't being used.

But every so once in a while someone from the city would move out to the country who had the money and the vision to restore the fields and the orchards to the way they used to be and it was one of these people that put an ad in the farm and garden section of Craigslist that Charles Morgan read: "Wanted: Someone to help restore my apple orchard. At least a month long project, and maybe two. Trees need LOTS of pruning. Ten dollars an hour plus meals and a place to stay for the duration. Experienced gardeners only need apply. Call 555-123-4567"

Charles Morgan called the number and found himself connected to Carlo who was a rich investment banker from the city who didn't get out to his farm much. Charles Morgan and Carlo hit off on the phone, and agreed on a scope of work and salary.

Then Carlo fedexed Charles Morgan his first paycheck and the keys to his farmhouse to stay in while he restored the orchard.

Could he prune the apple trees as well in the nude as when fully clothed? Yes, he could! There was perhaps a small price to pay in terms of several additional scratches from the raspberry bushes which were growing up interspersed among the trees of the orchard that he got on his bare legs that he wouldn't have gotten had he been wearing long pants or heavy coveralls. But by being in the nude, he moved more deliberately and so was able to avoid brushing against most of them, and the sharp, protruding branches of the apple trees as well. Furthermore, he did not fall prey to putting his foot in one of the numerous old woodchuck holes that were distributed amongst the orchard trees. He was more careful to see where he placed his feet, since they were bare, than he would have been had he been wearing shoes or boots. Thus, in all likelihood, being nude actually helped him to avoid gardening mishaps on the orchard renovation job. A twisted or broken ankle from plunging an unsuspecting foot into a woodchuck hole because one wasn't looking where one was going was no fun, and the thought of what would have happened had he not avoided them entered his mind more than once as he skillfully avoided them on a regular basis by virtue of the enhanced sensitivity to his surroundings that he got from being in the nude. All in all, it was a wonderful job, and he felt attuned to the true blue of sky and the many green spirits which were around him in the orchard as he went about his work. He used hand saws and chain saws and clippers and loaded up three or four pickup truck loads of dead wood every day and brought it in to the back dooryard where he made bonfire every night. And under his caring hand and by virtue of his loving heart ("Every garden starts with a loving heart.") he was able to transform that run-down, neglected, has-been orchard into a shining beacon of hope for the future of apples and apple growing that would have made Johnny Appleseed proud and several of the nearby roadside fruit stand proprietors newly desirous of an acquaintance with its owner.

Since it was Fall, after tending to the apple trees, the leaves near the house needed to be raked. Raking leaves was a job Charles Morgan thoroughly enjoyed. By raking leaves manually, with a good stout rake, you could do a better job than you could with a leaf blower. And instead of wasting gas and emitting toxic vapors and who knew how many decibels of noise[8], you exercised the body (pronounced 'bod-ee') and breathed in good, healthy, fresh air, with just the right note of Fall crispness in it. Oh yes it was heaven to rake leaves. It was divine! And to do it in the nude was so much more fun! But there are some people who are too lazy to enjoy this pastime. They want the instant gratification that a leaf blower gives them. They want their lawns done in 30 minutes, whereas it took Charles Morgan an hour and a half.

So what? An extra hour! All that hurry up and go just so you could shuffle back to the couch and watch tv, perhaps? What was the point? Charles Morgan would never join that club. He had his scruples. Oh yes, he had principles that he lived by. And he was not one to do something just because everybody else was doing it. And he was not one to do something which destroyed the natural wholesome and sacredness of Life, which almost anything which had to do with internal combustion engines seemed to do by definition. And wasn't it obvious that using those big noisy rider lawn mowers to vacuum and/or mulch the leaves, like some people do, or using those noisy backpack blowers to blow them from place to place (and then back again!) your hearing was going to be damaged? Even with ear protectors?

After getting all the fall chores done around the beautiful old falling down farm, and with Winter coming soon, Charles Morgan decided he would hitchhike down to New Jersey to see Saunders, and then head out to the Southwest.

17

The Bad President Hears The Nude Yardman On the Radio

Because of his constant practice of doing yard work in the nude, Charles Morgan had developed an adonis-like physique and became a paragon of physical fitness. He was tanned, lean and muscular without the grossly excessive muscular structure that professional body builders have. Because he was good look-ing, the Bad President hated him even more when he saw him on television, because as a good-looking nudist he attracted more people to his "cause". But one time he got the Bad President really mad was when the Bad President heard him on the radio, not the television.

NPR wanted to do a segment on the nude yard worker movement so it sent its ace correspondent, Sylvia Poggiloi, out to interview Charles Morgan, who taped him.

He said, on the air to millions and millions of people who listened to Fresh Air that night with Terry Gross: "It is the right of all people who like to garden to do it in the nude. They do so not to be exhibitionists or to impress other people one way or another. They do so because it makes them feel good. And if you'll try it, it will make you feel good, too. Any public official, especially the President of the United States, who would seek to punish someone for doing their gardening or yardwork in the nude is not thinking very clearly. There are 40 million home-owners in this country. They can't stop us if we all choose to exercise this basic human right. So go ahead, do it! It feels great!"

The mind of the Bad President seethed with rage after hearing this interview Charles Morgan gave with National Public Radio which his Press Secretary played for him. It boiled and hissed and steamed and fulminated and sent out nasty, foul-smelling vapors like a hot springs fumarole.

18

The Nude Yardman
Meets His Fate

The Vice President had proposed a three point action plan to deal with the Nude Yardman in his secret counsel to the Bad President. The first was that a federal grand jury be convened to indict Charles Morgan on a charge of violating Title 18 US Code Section 2383 "Rebellion or Insurrection", to wit:

"Whoever incites, sets on foot, assists, or engages in any rebellion or insurrection against the authority of the United States or the laws thereof, or gives aid or comfort thereto, shall be fined under this title or imprisoned not more than ten years, or both; and shall be incapable of holding any office under the United States."

The second was that nude yard work would be designated a new type of terrorist activity by the Bad President in a secret executive order, which would of course be eloquently drafted in strict legalese by John Yodeleeheehoo.

And the third was that Charles Morgan be arrested and held indefinitely (or as close to indefinitely as possible) under the Patriot Act and its successors for his seditious and terrorist activities.

"Ha Ha!" That ought to fix him, thought the Bad President.

So that's what they did. John Yodeleeheewho was pulled off his orchid projects and picture straightening routines long enough to a write a hastily composed executive order proclaiming clothing optional yard work a clear and present danger to the nation, an exquisite lucubration requiring mental gymnastics of truly Olympian magnitude, perhaps his magnum opus. A federal grand jury was convened in Dallas, Texas where it was thought the local population would be the most hostile to the crazy liberal idea of walking around outdoors naked. It was also the last place where the government had actual knowledge of Charles Morgan's teaching nude yardworking to impressionable young people, impressionable old people and others in between, Texans all. These people were found and rounded up just like stray steers in a cattle drive and threatened to be held as material witnesses if they did not testify truthfully to the grand jury about his activities, specifically his teaching them to disobey the local public indecency laws, which as luck would have it were rather strict in that part of Texas. Since the local ordinances were made under the authority of the county and the county took its authority from the State and the State took its authority from the United States, the non-stop teaching of activities which were against the local laws could be seen as an act of rebellion against the United States, at least in theory. Whether or not it would hold up remained to be seen. But in any event, a proper trial might be years down the road and in the meanwhile, Charles Morgan could be put on ice and his movement would dissipate away like the morning fog on the Texas prairie, it was hoped.

The Bad President reveled in the power he had as President which could be seen by the way he smirked and strutted around the White House. His father had been a politician and had taught him all the tricks of the trade: how to sit idly by and pretend not to notice (ho-hum!) while your friends got skewered in the press, how to add chummy little friendly-sounding handwritten notes at the bottom of formal, unfriendly letters to make it look like you were taking a personal interest in things (but really weren't!), how to send get well cards to your enemies, how to count on the natural venality and crookedness of others in power, and all sorts of other subterfuges and stratagems. He didn't even have to remember them all! He simply had to call his dad up or ask him in person, because his dad took a personal interest in how his son was doing as president that he often dropped in at the White House for visits, both announced and unannounced, and his dad would tell him. "Do this," he would say. Or "Don't do that!" Or "If I was in your shoes, here's what I'd do..." It was so great having such a great dad who could do all the work for you. It left him time to play with his daughter, and to go skeet shooting with his rich friends at all their private clubs. Why heck, he even got a chance to get drunk every once in a while! There were those who said that he enjoyed the work of campaigning for office and was good at it more than the work of actually being in office. But the truth be known, he hadn't actually had to do all that much work to get into office, either. Existing educational credentials necessary for a credible candidacy? Those fancy Eastern schools had let him in simply because his dad had gone there. Missing parts of his public service record? Well, it wasn't fault that the military lost crucial pieces of paperwork every once in a while! Party affiliation? That was easy! He was a member of that grand old party where people voted for you no matter what your character was simply because you were rich and had money and thought that by voting for you you would help them get rich and have money, too. (The fact that it didn't actually work that way, snicker snicker, well, that wasn't his fault!) And if all else failed, and the voters decided to vote for someone else, despite all those good and excellent reasons for voting for him, well, heck, his friends and relatives would just jigger the election results, that's all.... Oh my gosh! Did I say that?

The idea that Charles Morgan was soon going to be skewered legally filled him with intense pleasure.

There is an old saying "You can indict a ham sandwich" which means that because the prosecution gets to present *all* the evidence, and *no* evidence is presented or can be rebutted by the defense, even an innocent party, even a party as innocent as a ham sandwich, can be indicted by a grand jury. Furthermore, because a grand jury is a captive audience that has to sit through days and days of mostly boring testimony from mostly hesitant witnesses, and persons of questionable character, who may or may not be receiving some form of compensation from the government for their testimony, and make really hard decisions concerning their credibility when they would really rather be home watching an episode of *Naked and Alone!,* or at the mall shopping for a new pair of shoes, makes the idea that they would labor over factual subtleties or inconsistencies rather unlikely. The legal standard for an indictment is a preponderance of the evidence, which means more likely than not that probable cause exists to believe the accused committed a crime, not proof beyond a reasonable doubt. And this is an easy standard to meet when no one is rebutting the evidence. So it was a foregone conclusion that Charles Morgan would be indicted once the justice department impaneled a grand jury to do so.

After the indictment was returned, the Bad President called the Attorney General into his office.

"Let's put an APB on him," the Bad President said.

"You mean you want us to put out an APB to every single solitary police department in America.… for a hitchhiker??? In the United States of America?" His Attorney General was dumbfounded.

"Yes, I do. I know it sounds a bit unusual, but I'm listening to my gut here, and my gut tells me that this guy is dangerous with a capital D. We need to bring him in and interrogate him. See who he's working for. See why he's trying to undermine the morals of this country!" The Bad President was sounding a little bit more paranoid than he usually did. His Cabinet was therefore worried about him. But he was the one who had been elected to the highest office in the land with 81 million votes a second time around, so they had to listen to him. Mostly.

"OK," said the attorney general. "I'll do it."

So an APB went out for Charles Morgan which had his picture on it taken from a television interview he had given to

KQED in San Francisco. The APB said he could probably be found hitchhiking. The good state troopers and sheriff's deputies of the nation shot their eyebrows up at the APB. But they soon started stopping hitchhikers and asking them who they were while looking for Charles Morgan. It took about a week, but they finally found him. He was arrested on a section of Interstate 40 near Little Rock and taken to the federal detention facility in Forrest City, Arkansas. Many of the inmates recognized him. They sent letters home to their wives and friends telling them that the nude yardman himself had been locked up with them, thinking that being locked up with a famous personage like them made them kinda more famous, too. Their friends and family members alerted others. Eventually the press was alerted and queried the Bureau of Prisons who replied yes, they did have Charles Morgan Prendergast in their custody.

'What was the charge he was being held on', the reporters with all the nation's finest newspapers and radio and television stations asked. "Well, we don't have that information, replied the Bureau of Prisons, which didn't like to give out information in the first place, even public information that they were supposed to give out. 'Contact the Justice Department in Washington. They'll be able to answer all your questions."

So the reporters at all the finest newspapers and radio and television stations across the country contacted the Justice Department and they were given the royal run around. No, they would not be told what charge Charles Morgan Prendergast was being held on. The Patriot Act and its extensions let them keep people in custody without charges, didn't they know that? "Aha! Said the alert members of the press. They are holding him on national security grounds! WTF? Charles Morgan Prendergast? The nude yardman? On national security grounds? Why he's not a national security threat!!! It must be that the nude yardworker movement has irritated that prudish president of ours who has locked him up on a bogus pretext of some sort or another!

So, being hardworking devoted members of their profession, and loving their country as much as a bear loves honey, and as much as the Sons of Liberty loved their country back in the days of George Washington and Benjamin Franklin, they began to write a whole series of articles, special exposes, interviews, and documentaries about the nude yardman's many exploits, and the growth of the nude yard worker movement in the country. This publicity campaign which filled the pages of the newspapers and magazines, and took up hours and hours of television and radio news time really caught on with the public, who didn't like the idea of Americans being locked up for no reason, oh no siree! Soon, the size and intensity of the animosity which was directed at the Bad President and his government really got under the skin of the Bad President.

"You see!" he shouted. "I knew he was trying to ruin this country! Look at how he has gotten everybody all riled up about his being arrested! And I arrested him for the good of the country! Gee whiz! No good deed goes unpunished," he said. But the Bad President's karma was finally catching up with him, as it always does. And soon it would REALLY catch up with him.

Membership in the nude yard worker movement increased 1,756% after Charles Morgan got thrown in jail. In the classic sense of the word, he became a martyr for the movement. The people of the United States hated the Bad President for throwing the happy, smiling young man in the clink when all he had done was to say that people ought to be able to do their yard work in the nude if they wanted to. Buxom mothers of 3, 4 and 5 children, as well as buxom mothers with other numbers of children and buxom ladies with out any children at all sympathized with the Nude Yard Man, as did beautiful ladies who weren't so buxom. So did hard-working businessmen, train conductors, telephone operators, ship builders, policemen, firefighters, college professors, construction workers, and shop owners. In Charles Morgan they could see the quiet rebel energy in themselves, the special energy they had quietly, secretly nurtured all those years without using. They could see that Charles Morgan was doing a sacred duty, like the monk in Tianamen Square who had stood up before the tank, or like the mothers in the Plaza in Argentina who held up pictures of their children who had been officially "disappeared". His work was their work they decided spontaneously, and his world was the kind of world they wanted to live in. And so all over the country, the nude yard worker movement gathered momentum. Phone started chiming, email inboxes started filling and long dormant fax machines started humming with articles, old and new. Offices got leased and lobbyists got hired. Bumper stickers and buttons and yard signs were produced, and started appearing everywhere. People went about their every day, ordinary business as they had always done, but at night when they got home, they devoted their energy to helping the nude yard worker movement. They gathered in coffee shops and book clubs and discussion groups at each others' houses to share their feelings, and their enthusiasm. They discussed nudity in general, and on this topic they realized how much they knew, and how ignorant they were all at the same time.

One senile old man who had grudgingly accompanied his wife to an evening discussion group declared that he had never been nude and thought it was all a bunch of nonsense. His wife glared at him and called him an old curmudgeon. "Henry, you've never been anything other than an old curmudgeon," she said. "I am not an old curmudgeon," he shot back. "How would you know if I've ever been nude?"

The prosecutor who was put in charge of prosecuting his case questioned Charles Morgan in the interview room after they brought him to the detention center.

"So, who are you working for? Hmm? The Russkies? The Chinese?" he asked. "You better answer me, otherwise you'll leave here in a box."

"Dude, I'm not working for anybody. I'm just gardening without any clothes on."

"Oh, I know all about you *gardeners*. You pretend to be so gentle, and so loving and so concerned, but underneath that pusillanimous exterior you're savage beasts! What about weeds? What about beetles? What about the deadly, ingenious methods you dream up to exterminate them? But the energy and careful plotting it takes to kill them cold-heartedly doesn't really end there, does it? It sometimes extends to people too, doesn't it? For instance anyone who threatens your beloved plants? Why I once saw an Irish lady, completely civilized, genteel, and well-mannered in all other respects, take up the wooden handles of a hot hibachi and chase her brother around the backyard with it and then throw the glowing coals at him simply because he had placed the hibachi too close to her beloved grapevine and had singed some of its leaves. Now some allowance must be made for the fact that she was Irish, but in the main it was the gardener in her that made her violently attack her brother. When she finally threw it, the hot coals bounced off him he was running so fast away from her and no harm was done as they spilled off him onto the ground but still and all it scared the bejesus out of him to have his loving sister running around after him with a hibachi full of hot coals as if possessed by a demon over the fact that he had merely carelessly located his hibachi in a place that threatened her beloved grapevine. Oh yes, it took him a long time to get over that. Not that he ever started another barbecue on the picnic table under the grapevine, mind you. Oh no, that he never did that. Her antics were effective in eliminating that problem."

"And what about Ghislaine Marchaad the murdered French socialite. In her case it wasn't the butler who did it but the estate *gardener*. A particularly heinous crime, the talk of Paris high society for months back in 1991. Did he use an axe? A meat cleaver? No, he did her in with a garden shovel!"

That conversation didn't go very far because Charles Morgan couldn't convince the overzealous prosecutor, who figured he was going to score *beau coup* brownie points for prosecuting the administration's public enemy number one, that he wasn't working for anybody other than himself. And that the people who followed him were gardening and doing yardwork in the buff were doing it because they enjoyed doing it, not because anybody was forcing them to.

The authorities confiscated his cellphone and looked at all his text messages and voice calls and investigated each and every one of the people on his contact list in an effort to find some malign influence, some nefarious foreign agency behind the so-called nude yardworker movement. But of course they couldn't. And when they got to Saunders, they hit a real dead end, because trying to track down Saunders, who was the nude yardman's best friend, was like trying to get your hands around smoke. It just couldn't be done. They weren't going to issue *two* APB's for every hitchhiker in the nation!

While he was in the detention center Charles Morgan got to read the prison magazines and newspapers and was surprised to learn that the nude yardworking movement was catching on all over the place." Wow!" he said to himself. "Did I do that?"

One day Charles Morgan received a letter while he was in prison. It was from his friend Mary. It said:

"Dear Charles,

I just want you to know that I love you no matter what you did and that I am waiting for you to come back home. And that I'll wait forever if I have to.

Your best friend forever,

Mary"

Charles Morgan wept when he read the letter. Like he hadn't wept in years.

And Charles Morgan also got a letter from Morgan LeFey, I mean Mistress Margaret, I mean Magic Margaret or whatever her name was out in Utah. It said:

"Dear Charles Morgan,

I heard you were in jail and I wanted to write to you. Those weeks with you that you spent as my love slave were the most fun I have ever had in my life. I often think of you with your golden hair and perfect bronze body and remember those days fondly. I know you are never going to come back to your Queen, to surrender yourself under her again, but I wish you well in your nude yardworking endeavors and hope they let you out of jail soon. Imagine my surprise when I saw your picture in the paper when they were putting you in jail.

Your favorite dominatrix,

Margaret"

"Dominatrix!" snorted Charles Morgan, thinking the girl must still have a screw loose, despite his efforts to try to help her.

Bubba, his big friend and roommate in prison who kept him out of trouble and protected him because he liked him, (no, not in *that* sort of way!), and who occupied the lower bunk in his cell used his toes to nudge the top bunk and said, "Yo, what did you say?"

Charles Morgan leaned over and looked down. "Sorry Bubba. I was just reading this letter from a girl who I had what in retrospect was an absolutely calamitous affair with. Calamitous. She thinks she's a dominatrix. But I think she's just lonely."

"A dominatrix? Well give me her number, man! I'm due outta here in a few weeks," Bubba said. He had heard about dominatrixes and was curious about them.

"You won't mind being chained up in her basement for weeks on end, and being fed nothing but bread and water, and the occasional veggie burger?

"Hell, no!" said Bubba enthusiastically. "What are guys for?"

"Well, there's that," said Charles Morgan. He sighed. Then he said "OK, I'll find it for you before you leave."

Tom, the nude yardman's father, liked to bet on sports games, football, basketball, baseball, you name it. One day, when he thought it might be getting a little out of control, he said to his brother Bartholomew, "I'm going to kill myself if I don't stop gambling." Well he didn't kill himself and he didn't stop gambling. So that was just another example of how Tom exaggerated. Everything he said was an exaggeration. Well, okay, you caught me! Obviously that's an exaggeration! Not everything he said was an exaggeration. But if you listened to him, most things he said *were* exaggerations. And if an AI program analyzed his speech and attempted to duplicate it it would exaggerate, too. If it didn't, well, a person who knew Tom, would say, "That isn't Tom speaking!"

Lots of people exaggerate when they speak, in fact an awful lot. So Tom's habit wasn't that uncommon. Neither was his gambling habit. They were just little idiosyncrasies of his that didn't really matter or not whether he would get to heaven. Whether he got to heaven depended on weightier issues, like whether he cheated on his wife, or was unkind to stray dogs, or honked his horn at a little old lady crossing the street, or forgot to make his bed in the morning. No, I'm kidding! Everybody knows those things don't matter either. But there are some things that do matter, and if a person listens to their conscience they know what they are.

Tom listened to his conscience and was a good man. In fact if Heaven assigned a social credit score to Tom, it would be very high.

So he, too, wrote his son. As a matter of duty and conscience. But the letter never got to him. The Bureau of Prisons does not like to let prisoners communicate with each other via the US Mail. Some of the time they open such letters and file them in their dossiers. Most of the time they just throw them away.

19

Charles Morgan Goes To Court

Charles Morgan was found guilty by a lower court but he appealed his case and it was taken up by the federal appeals case rather quickly, given its obvious significance. When the day came, Charles Morgan argued his own defense.

This is what he said on the day he stood up in front of the packed courtroom:

"There is a man in Japan who has spina bifida who walks on his hands to perform *kabuki*. There is a girl Africa who has no arms who uses her toes to hold a paint brush so she can paint. Her paintings are beautiful. There is a quadriplegic diver with only a torso who wiggles down the diving board by himself and dives from 7 meters straight into the water and bobs up to the surface without swimming. Different people in different parts of the world express themselves in different ways *against impossible odds.* Doing yard work in the nude is how I express myself, and I am driven to do so by something deep inside me. Isn't that my First Amendment right in these United States? I think you have to admit that it is. I am harming no one. This is not injurious speech."

The otherwise stoic faces of the 9 grave magistrates on the 5th Circuit Court of Appeals *en banc* panel blushed slightly as they heard this argument from the young pro se litigant in front of them who was obviously not a professional litigant, and looked like he sincerely believed in what he was saying. Some of them appeared to busy themselves with their papers, others looked at the clock, others yawned, and appeared to stare into space with a far off look. Yes, it was true. This did appear to be the young man's right. Given previous cases involving the rights of belly dancers and exotic dancers to perform erotic dances for pay, they could hardly make gardening in the nude illegal, any more than they could make howling at the moon illegal, which wouldn't fall under the public nuisance category unless you did it under your neighbor's window at 3 am. Perhaps everybody in the country had been caught off guard with how rapidly the fad had developed but notwithstanding that, looking at this man's case *as an individual,* it was clear he was not outside of his First Amendment bounds (even though the Great State of Texas said that he was outside of the bounds set by the indecency statutes of that State). Now legally the slight difference between Charles Morgan's activity and the proclivities of nudists in a private nudist resort were of interest in seeing where the proper boundaries were, but it could not be said that people were gardening in the nude on public property. By and large people were gardening in the nude on their own properties. And *if they were* gardening in the nude on public property, to make an artistic or social statement, they probably had an even bigger right to do so without any clothes on than when they were in their own backyard. Maybe. So the Justices with the bored and vacant looks on their faces were trying to think of something else pleasant to distract themselves with, like their daughter's upcoming wedding, or their new Hermes tie, or the upcoming bar association holiday social, because they knew they were going to have to sign off on Charles Morgan's naked gardening behavior eventually in their written decision, even though the Bad President and his cabal in the Justice Department were trying to make them put the kibosh on it. The bottom line was that humans had been dancing naked and walking around in the buff forever and it was hard to see what was wrong with it, if anything. The fact that The Bad President and his executive branch had a problem with it was an awkward, embarrassing aspect of this case, but it was an aside, really. The law in the form of its interpretation by the judicial branch had to look at the Big Picture. They were going to have to acquit the young man, and that meant the State of Texas and the Justice Department were going to be upset and embarrassed.

Oh well, you couldn't rule for the government all the time!

So the *en banc* panel was going to rule in Charles Morgan's behalf eventually, perhaps in a month or two's time, but intervening events took place before then which accelerated their decision.

20

The March on Washington

Like a snowball rolling downhill and inexorably getting larger and larger and larger with each passing moment, the nude yard worker movement gathered steam while the decision was pending. The movement climaxed, as all vitally important national movements do, with a march on Washington. The people wanted Charles Morgan Prendergast out of jail! Now!

The Bad President went down to Pennsylvania Avenue to meet the phalanx of nude yardworkers and people who believed it was their right to do it personally.

"Shoot them! Shoot them all," he screamed to the soldiers and secret service agents who were guarding the White House, for he had reached the limit of his endurance of this group of Americans who wanted to flaunt their nudeness, and who had no respect for the great tradition of wearing clothing in the long history of *his* great country.

The tank commander looked at his machine gunner who looked at the Army colonel in charge of the White House security detachment who looked at the Senior Secret Service Agent-in-Charge who looked at the White House Chief of Staff, who looked at the Chief Judge of the Supreme Court who had come down to the plaza in front of the White House to watch. Then they all looked at the President. Then they all looked at the crowd of bare-assed, marching Americans again, empty-handed in every respect except for a few signs that they were carrying. Then they looked at the President again.

"But we can't shoot them," complained the tank commander, finally. "They're totally unarmed! Who the heck wants to shoot a bunch of nude, unarmed Americans marching down Pennsylvania Avenue who just want the right to be able to exercise their First Amendment right and garden in the nude?"

"All they're doing is exercising their first amendment right to free speech and their Constitutional right to political association, Jack" said the Chief Justice of the Supreme Court to the President, who agreed that shooting into the crowd would be a terrible mistake.

The tank commander shook his head in disgust. Then he revved his engine and started to drive away. Everybody else relaxed a bit, and lowered their weapons, too.

"Well, if you won't shoot them, I will!" yelled the President, grabbing a gun from a soldier nearby him. The Senior Secret Service Agent in Charge was appalled. Here was a man who they had sworn to protect with their lives proposing to open fire on a group of totally unarmed Americans who were simply exercising their Constitutional rights peacefully and who were exactly like him in every respect except for the fact that they were nude.

"You can't do that. It would be un-American," said the Senior Secret Service Agent in Charge, wrestling the President to the ground before he could get a shot off. The Army Colonel came over and took the gun away from the President. "Yes, sir. It would be un-American. And we are not going to open fire on that crowd today, not today and not any day." He walked away and threw the gun to the soldier who it had been taken from. He didn't even salute the President, who he felt did not deserve a salute.

The crowd, which had paused while all this was going on, cheered at the sight of what was happening. They pored into the open gates of the White House, cheering with joy, waving their arms, saluting the astounded guards. The White House staff was completely dumbfounded at the arrival of these rightful claimants to The Throne, and, truth be known, well, maybe just a little bit happy and thrilled to see them there, even though they were marching into the place without any clothes on. Some of the marchers began to play frisbee. Some found the President's croquet set, and started to play croquet. From out of nowhere musical instruments appeared, and some of the erstwhile marchers struck up a tune here and there on the vast White House lawn with their guitars and mandolins. Others sat down to rest on the luxuriously soft grass, glad that they had not been shot; since no one had thought to bring along bandages and since no one had any clothes on, impromptu bandages for wounds probably would have been difficult to find. Still others went into the kitchen and brought out bottles of wine. It made all the members of the military glad to see all this happening. One of the Joint Chiefs of Staff, who were watching the events on television from the situation room in the Pentagon chuckled.

"I always knew that rascal was no good for this country," one of them said.

"Sick bastard," another one said, shaking his head, walking away from the viewscreen.

The President was led away by a small group of doctors in white laboratory coats, after first being tightly bound in a mummy-like straight-waist-jacket. Somehow it looked perfect on him. The Speaker of the House and the Secretary of State and the leader of the Senate had gotten together and decided that perhaps it was best if the President did not continue in his duties anymore, and the Chief Justice of the Supreme Court agreed. The Vice President was not consulted because of the simple fact that he was hiding at an Undisclosed Location, where he had gone in case the confrontation with the people demanding their right to do yard work in the nude had turned ugly. But he did not get a chance to succeed the President, which was a good thing, because all the members of Congress, who had watched the events unfold on television voted unanimously to impeach both the President and the Vice President that same day, in a hastily convened joint session of the House and Senate, where nary a word at odds was spoken between members of the two opposing parties, so ashamed was everybody at the President for being such a psycho nutcase and attempting to order the military to open fire on a bunch of defenseless, naked Americans. And so mad they were at the vice president for being in an undisclosed location all the time, they got rid of him, too, unanimously. That same day, they approved the passage of a Constitutional Amendment allowing the performance of gardening and yard work while in the nude. And the fair-minded Speaker of the House became a caretaker President until the next election. It was a complete and utter victory for the nude American citizens who had marched on the White House, and a complete and utter victory for the nude yardworker movement nationwide.

Ironically, the nude yardman was not there to savor the fruits of victory, the victory of the movement that he had helped start. He was still in prison. It was where his father had told him not to go, but it was where the strength of his convictions had carried him anyway. But he did watch it on the prison tv.

The nude yardman recognized some of his friends in the crowd on the CNN coverage of the event. There was Charlie who he had planted seedlings with in the forest in Upstate New York. And Leonard was there, too. He was happy to see them all on tv. Still, it would have been nice to have been with his friends on this glorious day. The nude yardman sighed.

Uncle Winkle was not able to watch the events on television either, the events which had been inspired by his young nephew, because he was in a remote part of the Amazon rain forest participating in a study to count the number of different insect species which fell into a huge tree canopy net one of his friends had set up. One of his friends, a principal investigator on the study, had invited him down to do some of the insect counting and since he had never been to the Amazon rain forest before, and since he was interested in entymology, and since he conjectured that he might be able to rub shoulders with some of the young graduate students of the opposite sex who were participating in the study, a conjecture that, as it turned out, had no basis in actual reality, he agreed to go. He learned about the dismissal of the President and the Constitutional Amendment from a letter his brother sent him. "Hot damn!" he said. "That little wiggle-worm finally did something!" In sympathy for the movement which was happening in the very civilized capital of his native North American country, Uncle Winkle tried for an hour or two, while in the jungle of a somewhat wild South American country, counting net-caught insects in the nude, but the hungry mosquitoes finally got to him, and he had to put his clothes on again. "Oh well, at least I tried," he said to himself.

21

The Aftermath

Unsurprisingly, the appeals court judges who had jurisdiction over Charles Morgan's case rendered a decision in his favor almost immediately after the embarrassing incident in Washington. An order went out to the Bureau of Prisons (BOP) that he be released without delay. The BOP bureaucrats don't like to release people from the prison system no matter what the circumstances, and it is known that in some cases individuals are held for years beyond their legitimate release dates, so they hemmed and hawed a little bit, before making a decision and complying. But in this case they figured the increased public scrutiny justified complying sooner rather than later so they sent a guard around to Charles Morgan's cell and told him to pack up his things, he was leaving.

He came out the doors of the federal detention center to a throng of reporters holding microphones and television cameras. Satellite link trucks were parked nearby with their dishes pointing to the sky, connecting to the world. He had his package of personal belongings with him and he didn't look all that different than he did when he first started on his journey hitchhiking.

They all gathered around him in anticipation of what he would say.

"Charles Morgan, do you have a statement for us?" one asked, holding his smartphone up with the microphone pointed toward him.

"Charles Morgan do you have anything to say?" another asked, in that breathless way reporters have of making everything seem so monumentally important.

Charles Morgan stopped for a moment and considered his thoughts and what he should say. He didn't much like being put in jail for nothing. On the other hand he just wanted to get home to Mary and be with her. He didn't want to stir up any trouble that would interfere with that, that's for sure. That wasn't his way. But he knew he had to say something. So he started out slowly, feeling his way along, trying to find the right words for the occasion which he could never in a thousand years have imagined would happen to him growing up in the quiet Southwest town where dreams came true.

"Thank you all for being here. It feels good to be out. Now consider this: why is it that the Goddess of Liberty is depicted bare-breasted in so many sculptures and paintings? As Delacroix painted her she is leading the people of the 1830 French Revolution with the French tri-color in one hand, a musket in the other, and her breasts bared to the world. So why is it that this old master painted her bare-breasted? Do you know? Hmm?....

It's because he wanted us to know that liberty was right there in front of our eyes... That there was nothing separating us from it.... *If we want it, we can take it.*"

"Tyrants are scared of human nakedness because a naked human has what could be called supernatural powers. Why do you think the ancient female warriors, the Amazons, went into battle naked? Why do you think the protest group Pussy Riot is so effective? Why do you think everybody is so scared of the Free the Nipple campaign?

Putting blankets on statutes and covering over paintings like they did in Washington recently was a sign that this government had lost its grip on reality. They imprisoned me because the movement I started was a threat to their power.

Ghandi said a nation is judged by how it treats its animals, but I say it is also judged by how it treats its plants. Plants are people too. Doing yardwork in the nude is a great way to connect with plants. It's a great way to experience Nature, and it is your birthright to be able to do it. No one should be imprisoned for doing it.

We are not throwing red paint on Impressionist paintings, we are not blocking highways, we are not breaking into buildings or smashing windows, we are merely exercising a little bit of freedom of spirit in our own backyards. Why is that a police matter? Why is that a problem for the State? Answer: It isn't!

Now if you'll excuse me I have to get back home to see somebody whom I haven't seen in a long time." And with that he started walking off across the prison parking lot towards the road which he knew from his smartphone map would take him to the highway where he could hitchhike home. Whew! What a month!

After Charles Morgan was released from jail, where his father had told him not to go, but where the force of his convictions had carried him anyway, he was lauded as a hero by his friends in the nude yard worker movement and in the nation as a whole, for his good-hearted exposure of the Bad President and the fuddy-duddiness of American nudity laws. On the steps of his house one morning a crowd gathered and asked him to make a pronouncement about the future, for they ascribed to him oracular powers to tell the future. Truth be known, he didn't think he had such powers. In his leading of the nude yard worker movement, a movement which sprang up completely naturally, and accidentally, he had accomplished all his objectives without knowing the future, but by simply following what he believed in. When the crowd that gathered asked him what he thought the near-term future would hold now that the bad President had been put away and a Constitutional amendment had been passed allowing yard work in the nude, Charles Morgan replied, "People will be happy." Then when they asked them what he thought would happen further on down the road, Charles Morgan at first didn't want to answer, because he didn't really know, but then he remembered a dream he had had the night before. "In the future it will be a crime for authors not to be able to command their subjects, for there will come a day when all authors and writers are employed by the State, and if an author does not get the people to do what it wants, they will be thrown in jail." The news crew that asked this question and everybody else who heard his answer was puzzled by this answer and thought that perhaps he was talking about the very far distant future, where indeed things like that might happen.

Later that night, when Charles Morgan was reading John Toland's *The Rising Sun*, he smiled when he saw Admiral Nimitz's assessment of the war after the Battle of Midway, in which the clever admiral, in response to a badgering press, had inserted a nice pun into his official statement.[9] 'I must be careful to study puns more closely', thought Charles Morgan, 'for it seems they might come in handy when answering questions from reporters.'

Congress didn't make it a Constitutional right to do anything else other than yard work in the nude. People still drove to work and walked down the street, and visited libraries, and bought the newspapers, and did all manner of other things with their clothes on. But after the Amendment passed it was not unusual at all to drive down the average suburban street and see 5 or 6 happy people busily planting their gardenias, mowing the lawn, pruning the trees, or raking the leaves in the nude. And if one watched closely, one could see little pirouettes, and high-spirited leaps, and other such things they did going on among the newly liberated populace, who it seemed had been yearning to do yard work in the nude for some time.

There were those who questioned the resort to a Constitutional remedy on this issue. "Nudity has been and always will be an issue for the States to decide on, without the interference of the federal government," they said. They wanted the Constitutional Amendment guaranteeing the right to do yard work in the nude overturned. But then there were those who pointed out that nudity was such a basic civil right, a human right that had been endowed by the Creator, and that gardening was such a good, wholesome activity, that nude yard working deserved special, Constitutional protection, especially since certain states, notably Rhode Island and Massachusetts had always been known for their prudishness, and might, out of spitefulness, outlaw the practice if left to themselves. Certainly Florida was not a state that one had to worry about in this regard, for Florida was the home of the topless doughnut shop, surely the basis of an 'eyeful' in the morning if ever there was one. And one did not have to worry about Nevada, either, for in a state where prostitution was legal, it could be taken for granted that nude yard workers would be sort of, well, *passe*. And though there were other states where the attitudes were such that one did not necessarily have to worry that the legislatures would do such a spiteful thing as outlawing nude yardworking, there were others that were borderline. So it was better to have a Constitutional Amendment, even if perhaps the circumstances under which it had been passed were a little unusual.

Needless to say, Charles Morgan, after having all this unexpected commotion in his life, deserved to live happily ever after, and he did. He married his true love Mary in a clothing-optional ceremony one fine sunny day at the local naturist retreat. Several of the marriage ceremony party-goers arrived via parachute, some via motorcycle. None had clothes on. Others arrived via stretch limousines wearing tuxedos and gowns. It was a clothing optional ceremony and everybody got along whether they were wearing clothes or not. It was quite a good wedding party. The two lovebirds settled down and had three children, who all grew up to be big and tall and strong, after arriving in the world without any clothes on, naturally. To provide for his family, the Nude Yardman took a job as the editor of a well-known gardening magazine, a job which he fulfilled for the rest of his god-given years with aplomb, because he was genuinely interested in the subject matter. And oh, one more thing. Shortly after the Good President who had been elected after the Bad President was taken away moved into the White House, he invited The Nude Yardman to a State Dinner one night to congratulate him on the success of his movement, to thank him for his help in getting rid of the Bad President, and to announce that he was going to give a full Presidential pardon to the Nude Yardman for his 'crimes'. His conviction for accessory to menacing would be completely erased. Charles Morgan arrived at the White House with Mary on his arm. But it so happened that the beautiful wife of the Good President, who had started a vegetable garden of her own on the White House grounds, invited him out to take a quick look at it first. And we all know what happened next.

22

1. ^In fact many modern researchers have come to the conclusion that lobsters, do in fact, have emotions. A simple Google search on the phrase "Do lobsters have emotions?" or "Are lobsters intelligent?" will prove very surprising to many readers. According to *Animals Australia*: "It is clear lobsters are unique creatures who have social bonds, feel pain and anxiety, and experience life in many of the same ways we do." Along with octopuses, they are considered highly intelligent and some can live to be 100 years old! And for those of you who don't think *octopuses* are intelligent, watch the internet video of the one sneaking out of his aquarium, walking across the lab floor to get some food, and then going back to his own tank and hopping back in to dupe his human captors

2. ^People for the Ethical Treatment of Animals

3. ^Just as at the time of the American revolution, brewing beer might have been called the quintessential American avocation.

4. ^See *Jesus Lived in India: His Unknown Life Before and After the Crucifixion* by Holger Kersten

5. ^Early in the 2000's Ted Turner, the founder of the CNN television network issued a strange piece of advice to Americans. He told them not to watch too much tv. It is believed that this was the only instance in the history of American business where the owner of a large conglomerate urged his customers not to use its purposefully-designed, physiochemically addicting product voluntarily.

6. ^One tuba player from Nebraska had such a good dream about playing tuba in a marching band nude that he convinced all the real life members of his high school band to March down main street in the next annual 'battle of the bands' in the buff. They were an instant hit, especially the drum majorettes, that soon there were other 'copy-cat' bands spring up around the country trying to imitate them.

7. ^ It is a little known fact that the internal security forces of America started thick dossiers on E.B White, the author of *Charlotte's Web*, and other harmless Americans back during J. Edgar Hoover's day. Like all government habits, the tradition continues today. They keep watch on *anybody* who is influential, even children's book authors, and people involved in nude yardworker movements. In fact, the more peace-loving a person is, the more they watch him or her. Kinda strange, isn't it? Makes you think peace is dangerous. And to them, it is!

8. ^The average gas-powered leaf blower puts out 80-90 decibels of noise. Sounds above 85 decibels can potentially cause severe damage to a person's hearing, especially with prolonged exposure. Not only this, but continued noise

exposure can leave people vulnerable to several other health concerns, as well.

9. ˆAfter 4 out of a total of 8 of Japan's aircraft carrier's had been destroyed in the battle of Midway, Admiral Chester Nimitz issued the following press release: "Pearl Harbour has now been partially avenged. Vengeance will not be complete until Japanese sea power is reduced to impotence. We have made substantial progress in that direction. Perhaps we will be forgiven if we claim that we are *midway* to that objective."